Antonio Marques Filho was born in 1967 in Brazil. He was a banker and has always worked in accounting and business administration. Currently, he is an entrepreneur in the party business and feels very fulfilled with what he does.

Despite a lifetime amid numbers, Antonio has always found refuge in letters and reading good books, especially fiction rich in suspense and mystery. The desire to write only came in adulthood, but the taste for reading, which began in childhood, accompanied him throughout his life. Already in adolescence, his gift for creating stories and entertaining everyone with great adventures was noticed, which he does with great dedication in his book: *Allan Smith and the Mysteries of the Forbidden Hills*.

I dedicate this book to my family, especially to my parents, my daughter, and especially my wife, who supported me so much.

Antonio Marques Filho

ALLAN SMITH AND THE MYSTERIES OF THE FORBIDDEN HILLS

AUSTIN MACAULEY PUBLISHERS™

LONDON * CAMBRIDGE * NEW YORK * SHARJAH

Ordering Information
Quantity sales: Special discounts are available on quantity purchases by corporations, associations, and others. For details, contact the publisher at the address below.

Publisher's Cataloging-in-Publication data
Filho, Antonio Marques
Allan Smith and the Mysteries of the Forbidden Hills

ISBN 9798891554252 (Paperback)
ISBN 9798891554269 (ePub e-book)

Library of Congress Control Number: 2024908782

www.austinmacauley.com/us

First Published 2024
Austin Macauley Publishers LLC
40 Wall Street, 33rd Floor, Suite 3302
New York, NY 10005
USA

mail-usa@austinmacauley.com
+1 (646) 5125767

I would like to thank my nephew, Filipi Marques Siqueira, for translating the Portuguese into English.

Table of Contents

Chapter I
The High School

In 1953, at the beginning of the school year, all students at Saint Inacio of Loyola Academy already knew about the difficult mission they would face: studying hard and following the harsh rules of regulations. This was more than a goal; it was an order. Those who did not follow the rules were severely punished with heavy paddles or had to kneel on corn kernels. And, if had to be, you would be expelled.

The academy building was a beautiful five-story building, with huge hallways filled with rooms. The bathrooms were luxurious and well-maintained. The canteen, in addition to being huge, was extremely clean with a wide variety of sweets and food. The courtyard was wide and gave access to the swimming pools, the soccer field, and the sports courts.

In front of the building was a beautiful garden with breathtaking flowers from all over the world. Poppies, amaryllis, and orchids were the favorite flowers of most of the girls. At the back of the building, a small forest with an immense variety of plants was not only used as a picnic area and gatherings of friends, but also as a perfect place to acquire knowledge about flora and its importance for the environment.

In this school, it had a rigorous division: the first two floors were for the boys; the two posterior ones, only for the girls; fifth was reserved for the library, the science laboratory, theater, arts, and the auditorium. Thus, it was only during recess that all students met to have lunch, talk, and exchange looks. It was an excellent educational institution, receiving, almost always, the award for best school institution in the state of Sao Paulo.

Every year, two very interesting events took place: the choice of the best athlete among the boys through a sports competition and a contest to elect the most beautiful and lovable girl in the school.

In the case of the boys, only those who were able to compete in the five difficult modalities of the championship were registered: running with obstacles, archery, pole vaulting, swimming and judo. In the case of girls, anyone who thought she was beautiful could apply, as they would be analyzed by a demanding and knowledgeable group. The number of registered candidates was huge, clearly showing that they were all very excited and confident about winning the so-dream title of 'most beautiful in the school'. The few boys who were interested in participating were already tense and uncomfortable, as they had already seen who was at the end of the line to sign up.

"I didn't like it at all!"

"Neither do I, Joca," agreed Fred.

"Stop worrying, you idiots! If you guys think Allan Smith will win again, you are very wrong! This year I will do everything to win. Even if I must cheat or make him not participate in the championship," said Jader, the school troublemaker, with an ironic smile.

Every year, the beauty contest started before the athletics championship. It was usually an arduous and complicated task for the judges since all the girls were beautiful, charming, and nice. And this time was no different…After three days of much dispute, the demanding stages eliminated many of the candidates, leaving only two finalists. The audience, who had been faithful since the first day, was euphoric, everyone wanted to see who would be chosen to take the sash and crown for being the most beautiful in the school.

"She is so beautiful!" Allan said with a passionate look.

"Which one?" Samuel, his best friend asked.

"The one on the right, the blonde with the blue eyes!"

"Ah…Her name is Jessica."

"She is the daughter of teacher Telma, who teaches science and history."

"I didn't know that, Samuel! I just know that I'm in love."

As they paraded once more, Allan, not holding anymore, climbed on the chair, smiled, and blew her a kiss. The girl blushed with embarrassment, but she smiled back at him too. Jader, also in love with the same girl, was angry at his rival's attitude.

"He is going to pay, I'm going to finish him off," he whispered.

Samuel, irritated by his best friend's attitude, pulled him down, calling his attention, "You're crazy, Allan! Do you want to be punished?"

"You're right, but I already told you that I'm in love. She reminds me of a picture of my mother in her girlhood!"

"Yes, I understand…But now behave and let's see the final result of the contest," Samuel replied.

Suddenly, the chairman of the jury committee stood up and began to publicize the result.

"Students, teachers, and guests, the jury has just elected the newest beauty queen. With five votes to two, the one who was elected is…"

"Ah, my heart is beating so fast!"

"Quiet, Allan, let's hear it."

"Miss Jessica!" finished the chairman.

Allan, who was paralyzed by emotion, was even more so after Jessica received the sash, crown, and bouquet of flowers, smiling at him.

Jader, biting himself with jealousy, got up immediately, and addressed Allan with harsh threats:

"Allan Smith, take your eyes off that girl…She's mine because I saw her first! And, if I hear that you have any funny ideas with her, I will finish you."

"Look here, you spoiled brat, first, the girl is not yours and she doesn't even know you exist! And second, if you're up for a fight, know that I'm not afraid of you!"

When things were already heating up between them, a teacher, who was nearby, asked them to calm down, as they were in danger of being expelled from the school. Given this, the two retired, each to one side. Jader, who was very angry and spiteful, left vowing to end his competitor in the five trials of the championship.

"You must be more careful with Jader! Despite being from our class, he doesn't like you since you defeated him in the final event of judo in the championship last year!"

"Yes, I know, Samuel, but I don't want to worry about that, but just think about the sweet smile of that beautiful girl."

The next day, the day before the boys' tournament began, Allan went into hiding during botany class hours and, without measuring the consequences, went to the garden in front of the school, chose the most beautiful flower he saw, and then ran to the upper floors to search for the room of your beloved.

Jader, watching all that, had a great idea. In a hurry, he ran to the principal's office with his two friends, Joca and Fred, to alert him of what was happening.

His intention was to have his great rival expelled or suspended to stay out of the competition and stay away from Jessica.

Samuel, who had also observed all that, could do nothing, just prayed that his colleague would not be caught by that thoughtless act.

Allan immediately found the room he was looking for. When he noticed that the teacher bent down to pick up a chalk that had fallen to the floor, he took the opportunity, quickly entering the room and handing the flower with a letter to the girl.

Jessica blushed again, thanked, and smiled, putting the letter in her pocket. Her friends died of envy, and the teacher, who saw nothing, continued the lesson.

When he was coming down, Allan was very surprised when he met the head of the school and the three boys who reported him.

"It's him, sir," said Jader pointing.

Very angry, the director ordered the three whistleblowers to return to botany class and only then warned the boy:

"Mr. Allan Smith, you know the rules of the school very well. No student should pass through the female sector…So I have no choice but to punish you!"

Allan, thinking quickly of a way out, reached into his pocket and said to the director, "Mr. Director, I am not coming from where you are thinking. I went to the fifth floor, in the library room, to get this scarf that I had forgotten there! I think I'm starting to get sick!"

"My dear friend, one of the first punishments at school is suspension and, if you continue to make a mistake, you will be expelled…You are a smart boy, but you did not convince me with this lame excuse! However, as you have not been caught in the act, but have been denounced, you will be punished with a paddle."

That day, Allan was severely punished. His right hand was completely swollen and, worse, he had to endure the laughter of his whistleblowers. But, even so, Jader was not satisfied, because what he wanted was to see his rival suspended from school.

***

Finally, the day so longed for by the boys arrived and, at that moment, there was no talk of anything other than the tournament. Many risked a guess and even bet who the new champion of the school would be.

Allan, with his hand still very sore, was about to leave the competition, but it was his friend who prevented him from taking that action.

"You can be sure that this is what they wanted most! Do not give this pleasure to Jader and his friends…Go and participate with your head held high. The important thing is not to win, but to compete! Don't forget you are still the best and you have a great chance of being the champion! I, just like every year, will count only on luck to win all stages!"

"All right! But stop being modest, Samuel, you, for me, are one of the best! Well then, let's go."

Only twenty boys signed up for the competition. The first stage, which was the hurdle race, was being considered the most important, as it would eliminate fifteen candidates at once. In the following trials, the last place would be eliminated definitively until the great champion was the only one left.

Anxious, all the competitors were already prepared for the start of the trial, which consisted of taking two laps around the soccer field. Then, they would go to the sports courts where they would jump the obstacles; then they would go for a walk around the woods and, finally, they would return, again, to the courts to cross the finish line.

With a whistle, the competition judge gave the start signal, and all the boys fired like crazy around the field. The trial was well disputed, everyone wanted to qualify in the top five, but at the end of the first two laps, many were already tired, with their mouths open.

When they reached the courts, the first five were: Jader, Samuel, Allan, Fred, and Joca. But when the obstacles were overtaken, Samuel took the lead, followed by his friend Allan, then Fred, Joca, and in fifth, Jader. They ran toward the woods, went around them and, when they were approaching the finish line, Jader was already the third, almost reaching the second, which was still Allan. But there was no way, the trial ended with Samuel in first, Allan in second, Jader in third, Fred in fourth, and Joca in fifth. All other competitors were disqualified only one of the top five would be the future champion.

Soon after, the second trial started: pole vaulting. Allan was concerned, as his hand still hurt a lot and it was a serious reason why he was not able to do it successfully. The height established was three meters, and the judge would determine who had the best performance.

The first chosen to jump was Fred. Clearly nervous, he ran and jumped, but it was perfect, and it got everyone's applause. The second chosen to jump was Jader. He focused, ran, and jumped, but he couldn't be as bright as his friend, as he bumped his back on the height meter. The third was Samuel, who was calm and confident, but just as he jumped, he dropped the height marker. Allan would be the fourth and everyone stopped to watch him. His hand appeared to be swollen; he couldn't close it, nor could he force himself to throw himself. Then he ran and, forcing the stick to the ground, gave a cry of pain, but managed to reach only the mark of two meters in height. It looked like it was over.

Samuel was very saddened by his friend's performance. He said a few words to comfort him because that was just a competition. Jader, laughing up to his ear, said to his friend Joca:

"Allan is in your hands, finish him off! If you do well in the jump, the idiot will be in last place and will not qualify. And more, if you do it, I'll pay for your snacks to the end of the month!"

"Okay, Jader! You can leave it to me. He will not pass this stage!" Everything was prepared. Joca, who was the fifth to jump, prepared himself and ran. However, the free snack, offered by the friend, did not leave his head. And as soon as he looked at Jader to give him one last thumbs-up, he tripped and fell badly to the floor. In addition to severely twisting his ankle, he had to be taken urgently to the hospital, as the fall cut his knee, and he had to take some stitches. Everyone was worried about him, except for Jader who just wanted to punch his nose.

The trial ended with Fred in first, Jader in second, Samuel in third, and Allan in fourth.

After helping Joca, the third trial could begin. The athlete would have to hit a fixed target using a bow and arrow. It seemed easy, but they would have to be very focused since all four competitors would need to be twenty meters from the target that was divided into four colored circular parts. The first, the one on the tip, was white and was worth ten points. In a row came green, which was worth twenty, the red was worth thirty, and the last, the one in the center, black, was worth forty points. Fred was chosen again to start. He concentrated, took aim, and fired. It didn't go so well, it hit the white color that was worth ten points. The second was Samuel. He took aim and hit the green color. The next was Allan and that was one of his favorite sports. However, his hand was not helping much; it was hard to hold the arrow, make a face like someone in pain, take aim, fire, and hit the black color, which was worth forty points. The last to fire was Jader, who, without any ceremony, gave Allan a dismissive smile. Then he took aim, fired, and hit the black color, thus managing to tie with his rival.

Just for the sake of classification, the judge ordered the two to repeat the trial. Allan took the bow and arrow, but, as he was already qualified for the next trial, he didn't want to force his hand too much. He aimed and hit the red color, which was worth thirty points. Jader, not wanting to miss that opportunity to come first, concentrated and took aim. When he saw that he had hit the color black, he was extremely convinced, and a great air of mockery took him.

Those who qualified for the swimming trial would be Jader, Allan, and Samuel.

The judge determined that the fourth and the last modalities would be disputed only on the next day. With that, the three athletes would have time to rest and prepare better. Jader did not like this at all, as his main opponent could take advantage of the situation.

***

The next day, Allan was more willing, and his hand was much better. I could now open and close it naturally without feeling pain. Samuel, who soon saw his friend's happiness, asked him:

"So, Allan, did your hand get better?"

"Yes, today it's much better!"

"Ah! So, Jader and I are lost as Super Allan is back!"

"Don't play like that. You are a very good competitor, Samuel!"

"Not as much as you…But be careful with Jader, he wants to win this championship anyway, even if he has to cheat!"

"Thanks for reminding me! I'll try to be very attentive."

The swimming trial was one of the most anticipated, both by the athletes and the fans who followed the championship. Athletes would need to swim freestyle also known as crawl and then come back in the butterfly style.

Allan has always been a great swimmer. From an early age, his father influenced him to practice this sport because he thought it was beautiful and healthy. So, he couldn't wait to start…Allan knew he had a good chance of winning.

17

The three were on their respective lanes, and Jader, knowing his rival's potential, tried to annoy him with unpleasant words. His offenses, however, had the opposite effect, since, as soon as the judge authorized it, Allan dived with such perfection that he left his competitors unfocused. It was incredible, with each stroke, Allan left Jader and Samuel far behind; he looked like a fish. He returned in the butterfly swim giving a sample of a lot of technique and agility. Seeing the audience enthusiastically applauding his victory, Allan was very happy but soon saddened to see that his friend Samuel was in third place, being then disqualified for the fifth and final trial. Seeing the sadness of his friend, he said, "Samuel, don't be like that, you did great! Of the twenty students who signed up, you came in third."

"Yes, Allan! I'm a little upset, but now I'm going to root for you! Keep your eyes open, Jader is untrustworthy."

The last trial was about to begin. And, as everyone had already predicted, the same finalists from last year would decide, again, in the judo match, who would be the champion. They were both great fighters; since childhood, they practiced this sport for some purpose Allan trained as a self-defense and had an excellent technique to dominate the opponent. But, unlike his rival, Jader liked to practice this type of fight to frighten anyone who stood against him and, also, to gain more and more reputation for being a violent boy.

All the students in the school wanted to watch the championship final. They were anxious and curious to see who would win the trial and to watch close combat with a lot of technique.

Judo is practiced and played barefoot. The judoka wears pants and a tunic of resistant fabric, called judogi or kimono. The tunic is held by an obi whose color indicates the athlete's graduation. And, at that moment, the two, who wore the much-desired black belt around their waist, were already prepared on a square platform, covered by the tatami.

Seeing that everything was in perfect order, the judge determined that the athlete who knocked the opponent on his back or immobilized him on the ground twice would win the fight.

Then the fight started. Jader made the first move, trying to surprise Allan. But there was no way; the rival's defense technique was incredible. Then, it was Allan's turn to try to surprise his opponent. The two grabbed each other trying to knock each other down. Seeing that the opponent was tough as nails,

Jader tried to apply blows to him not allowed in judo and was severely warned by the judge.

Allan always remembered his master's teachings…one of the most important was: let the opponent attack, furious, and use his own strength against himself and that is what happened…Jader, thirsty for revenge for remembering the defeat of the previous year, went up again, with all anger. Allan, who was pretending to be a fool, took his opponent by the shoulders and delivered a blow known as a sweep kick, which consisted of placing one leg behind the opponent and pushing him back. Jader was unable to balance himself, he fell backward to the ground losing the first stage of the fight.

The judge ordered a five-minute stop for the two athletes to have a glass of water and rest for a while before starting the second stage. In the meantime, Samuel ran to meet his friend and offered him a glass of juice. Jader, very irritated, asked his friend, Fred, to come urgently to the canteen.

"What Jader, will you buy me a snack?"

"This is no time for games, Fred! You know very well that if Allan takes me down again, he will win the fight."

"Yes, I know, but why are we going to the canteen?"

"I told you I would win this year even if it was cheating, and I have a plan…Take that pepper jar and throw it in my hands."

"But what do you intend to do?"

"In time you will see," said Jader, smiling.

Fred, without letting anyone know, did what his friend asked him to do. And, more than quickly, they returned to the combat site, as the judge was already waiting to restart the test.

Soon the second round began. Allan did not want to take too much risk, he was calm and knew that if he continued like this, the championship would once again be in his hands; then, wisely, he waited for the opponent to come like crazy to try to surprise him again. Jader didn't think twice, grabbed his opponent by the tunic and, not wanting to miss that opportunity, did what he had planned.

Allan, with his eyes burning and unable to open them, tried to complain, but he was soon surprised by a sweep kick, the same blow that had made him win in the first stage, falling on his back to the ground. As soon as he got up, he immediately went to the judge to warn him of his opponent's dishonesty;

but being unable to prove anything, he had no choice but to take advantage of the five minutes of stoppage and go to the bathroom to clean his eyes.

Samuel went after his friend and asked him, "What happened, Allan?"

"That bastard passed something in my eyes, and I can't see anything!"

"Allan, remember that you once told me about blindfolded training in one of your judo classes?"

"Well remembered, Samuel!" That day, the teacher taught us to sense the opponent when he was close to attack.

"So put what you've learned into practice! Go there and finish that bastard."

It was the last round of the fight. Whoever won would take the title of champion. The judge called the two and gave the authorization to restart the fight. Until that moment, Allan was unable to open his eyes or see, but after he had talked to his friend, he was calm and concentrated. Jader, who laughed a lot, tried to ridicule his opponent and made gestures about who was already the champion. Fred, who was in the crowd, shouted, "Finish with this idiot!"

"You can leave it to me, Fred. This will be for you and Joca," he replied, giving his friend a thumbs-up and going at his opponent like crazy.

But Allan, who sensed his opponent approaching, grabbed his arms, with much reflex and technique, giving him a blow known as a balloon. Jader totally lost control, rolled in the air, and fell badly on his back, being paralyzed on the floor without knowing whether he was ashamed or angry. The fact is that he had lost the championship, for the second year in a row, to his biggest rival—and he had his eyes closed.

Everyone in attendance fervently applauded Allan's technique and immediately embraced and greeted the athlete who entered history as the only one to win, twice in a row, the difficult college tournament.

A platform with three divisions was set up to receive and reward the first, second, and third-place competitors. Below was Samuel, in the middle, Jader, and on the top, Allan, who climbed up with some difficulty and only after receiving the trophy and the champion belt did, he manage to open his eyes definitively, being immensely happy to see Jessica, the girl of his dreams, in the middle of the audience, smiling at him. That, without a doubt, was his best prize.

Chapter II
A Difficult Decision

The weeks leading up to the mid-year school holidays made students at the Santo Inacio de Loyola school wonder what their fate would be in the long-dreamed school recess.

The most euphoric talked about traveling, going to the amusement park, the circus, the zoo, etc. Others, less enthusiastic, just wanted to rest and enjoy the family.

Samuel seemed the most outraged in the class. Even so, he tried to hide the frustration of not being able to enjoy the good things in his city or travel. The financial situation of his father, who had just lost his job, was complicated.

The next day, not enduring such sadness, Samuel asked his best friend:

"So, Allan, are you going somewhere on vacation?"

"Yes," replied a little thoughtfully. "But I still haven't decided where I will go."

"Why?" Samuel asked.

"My paternal grandparents want me to go to London, where they live…"

"Wow! Do they live there? I didn't know that you are of English descent!"

"I am. My father is English and came to Brazil a lot for business. One day, he met my mother, right after staying at a hotel here in Sao Paulo where she worked as a receptionist. It was love at first sight. They dated and moved to London as soon as they got married. My mother became pregnant and, even so, she helped my father manage the business, which by the way was doing very well. However, the news that the Second World War was going to break out and that Germany, led by Hitler, would try to invade London with all its war power, made my parents decide to live here in Brazil to start a new life and give more tranquility to the future baby that was about to arrive, which, in this case, is me! Despite the sadness, thank God nothing happened to my paternal grandparents during the five years of war. But those who were satisfied with my parents coming here were my maternal grandparents, who live on a beautiful farm in the countryside of Minas Gerais and want me to go on vacation there too."

"Wow, you are so lucky!" exclaimed Samuel.

"Why?"

"Now, who wouldn't want to have that doubt to worry about? One that London must be beautiful with its castles, carriages, princes and princesses. But also, who would not like to spend their holidays on a farm in the countryside of Minas Gerais, with all that nature, fresh air, rivers to fish, trees to climb, harvest fruit, and milk the cows and ride horses on beautiful trails. Ah…Without a doubt, it would be a great trip!"

"Well…But that's not the problem! I didn't want to hurt any of them!"

"And how long will take you to resolve this difficult issue?"

"As soon as possible, maybe tomorrow," said Allan.

The next day, the two friends met at school, and Samuel was immediately asking:

"So, Allan, how was it from yesterday to today?"

"I did well, thanks! I'm just a little worried."

"And why?" Samuel asked interested.

"My mother said that my maternal grandparents and uncles are all very sad. They may have to sell the farm in a while. So, I ended up deciding to go there on vacation, because, in addition to bringing a little joy to them, it may be the last time I will go to that wonderful place."

"I'm sorry for your grandparents, but I'm glad you decided your destiny. I, however, have no place to go, but I will try to have fun as much as I can," said Samuel with his head down.

"Samuel, why don't you go to the farm with me? My grandparents and uncles would love to meet you and don't worry, they are very hospitable, and the house is quite big with several rooms…We're going to have a lot of fun!"

"Yeah, I accept! But I must know if my parents agree. And you ask your mother if you can take a friend. Anyway, I'm very happy that you invited me. I would love to meet your grandparents and uncles and have a lot of fun!! I hope my parents let me go."

"Don't worry, Samuel, I have an idea! Today, when I speak to my mother, I'm going to ask her to come over to her house to make the invitation in person. I don't think your parents will deny it."

"Cool, Allan! I will be waiting for you tonight and I will love that our parents become friends."

When night arrived, the Smith family went to Samuel's house. He himself answered the door, very satisfied, saying:

"Come in soon, please, Mr. and Mrs. Smith. I'm Samuel, Allan's friend, and these are my parents, Paulo Teixeira and Rita Teixeira…Father, Mother, this is Allan, my school friend that I mentioned."

"It's a pleasure, let's go in and bring a coffee for visitors, Rita. But to what do we owe the honor?" Mr. Paulo asked.

"Well. My son is going to go on vacation to my parent's farm, in the countryside of Minas Gerais, and I would very much like Samuel to go with him. Then he asked me to come in person with my husband to make the invitation," explained Mrs. Julia Smith.

"Well, that's fine by me! And his mother had already agreed; we just want him to promise us that he will behave," replied Mr. Paulo looking seriously at his son.

"I promise, Dad! I will behave very well." Samuel was very happy with his father's decision. And he would really keep his promise to behave so as not to displease him. Then he called Allan to play in his room.

After they had their coffee, Mr. Paulo, awkwardly, said, "Mr. and Mrs. Smith, as I said before, my wife and I have authorized our son to go along, but I am in a difficult and delicate situation. I lost my job, and I can't afford the expenses."

"Don't worry about it…Your son will be well received, and the expenses for tickets, food, and everything else will be on us. And what did you work with?"

"I worked at a fabric factory, Mr. Richard. There I headed the entire production sector. The final word on the quality of all the fabrics manufactured was entirely my responsibility. However, the factory got into debt and had to close its doors."

"Interesting, it seems like a coincidence! My wife and I have a clothing factory, a clothing factory. We are doing well in business, but we want to improve our export sales. In a few days, I will go to London where I must close contracts with big stores. If all goes well, I will need a person who understands fabric quality. But I will give you the answer as soon as I return from the trip…"

"And who will take care of your company while you are away?" Mrs. Rita asked.

"My wife, she will take the boys to the farm, give the family a hug, and return to Sao Paulo. As soon as she returns, I will leave for London."
At the end of the night, the two families said goodbye, wishing everyone a happy trip.

Chapter III
The Trip

On the last day of school, all students were very anxious to hear the school signal ring and jump and sing with joy, as they would have thirty days' worth of vacation. With about ten minutes to go before class ended, the teacher Telma, who taught science and history subjects, informed everyone in Allan's classroom that she was concerned about each student's academic performance. She then asked them to bring, after the holidays, an assignment of these subjects, because it was the class that had the lowest grades in the school. The student would have a free choice of theme and the best assignment would give, in addition to the points, a Saturday in the best amusement park in the city, free of any expense, with the right to a snack and a delicious ice cream.

Allan was the student who was most interested in the task, because, in addition to being aware that he needed to improve his grades, he knew that the teacher was the mother of the girl he was in love with. And not enduring so much curiosity, asked, "Teacher Telma, besides you and the student, will other people go on this tour?"

"I don't think so. Ah…Yes, I will also take my daughter, because I will not leave her alone."

Another who was very interested in the activity was Jader, who also was dying of love for the same girl.

The moment the teacher finished the assignment, the bell rang, and all the students left euphoric and happy because the vacation was starting.

The only ones to say goodbye to the teacher were Allan and Samuel. She, admiring the education of the two boys, asked them:

"Are you two going to travel?"

"Yes, ma'am, we will go to my grandparents' farm, in the countryside of Minas Gerais," replied Allan.

"But it seems that you are not in a hurry."

"It's just that we will only go tomorrow. Today we will just pack our bags," concluded Allan.

"Since you're not in a hurry, could you two help me get these books to the car?"

"Yes ma'am! We would be happy to help. I'll take the books and you, Samuel, take the notebooks."

"Thank you very much! Then let's go!"

When they got to the car, Allan felt his heart pounding when he saw that Jessica was waiting for her mother.

"Hello, Jessica, this is Allan, and this is Samuel. I'm glad they helped me bring the material, it was so heavy."

The girl blushed, but responded with great politeness:

"Nice to meet you, how are you?"

"Very well," the two replied together.

Even though he was shaking and pale with emotion, Allan continued to speak, "You know, you look a lot like your mother, and you're very kind, Jessica! Samuel and I are helping, because she would not be able to handle all this weight alone."

"And it was a great help! And, since you were so kind, how about a ride?" Mrs. Telma offered.

"No, thanks…No need to worry," replied Allan.

"Yes, we will accept," said Samuel. "The sooner we get home, the more time we have to pack."

Allan was happy with his friend's attitude, as he knew he had done it with the intention of helping him.

After they explained where they lived, everyone got in the car and left. Allan, who was in the back seat with his friend, could not take his eyes off Jessica, who was in the front with her mother. And after a few minutes, he exclaimed,

"Wow. You are a very good driver!"

"Thank you, Allan! Since my husband passed away, I have been forced to learn several things in life."

"Ah, Mrs. Telma, you can drop me off at the next corner, I live right there," said Samuel. "And thank you very much for the ride!"

"You're welcome. Have a nice vacation and have a great trip."

"Samuel, try not to be late. Don't forget that we will be leaving early, tomorrow," Allan said.

After a few minutes, the teacher arrived at Allan's house and said,

"So, this is where you live?"

"Yes, and there is my mother waiting for me."

"How strange, it seems that I know her!"

"Mom, this is my teacher Telma, and her daughter Jessica. They offered me a ride."

"Telma, do you remember me? It's me Julia; we worked together at the hotel."

"Yes, of course I remember! Good to meet you after so many years."

"So, let's go in and have some delicious coffee. Son, take this money and go with your friend Jessica to buy some cookies. My friend and I have a lot of things to remember."

Allan was very happy with his mother's request. It was the first time that I had the opportunity to be alone with Jessica. But, contrary to what he always was, he was shy and embarrassed; emotion kept him silent.

The girl then started talking,

"Allan, I still haven't had the opportunity to congratulate you on the beautiful championship. You were just brilliant!"

"Thanks, you were also wonderful in the beauty contest; deserved to win and…Can I ask you something?"

"Yes," replied the girl.

"Did you read the letter I gave you that time in your classroom?"

"No. That day, just after you left the room, one of the girls commented to the teacher. Then she searched me, found the note, and tore it up. But I was enchanted with the flower, it was beautiful, the most beautiful I have ever seen! But I think you took a lot of risks; you could have been expelled!"

When the two were about to ask each other more questions, they noticed that they were already in front of the bakery. Only when they left did Jessica ask,

"Won't you tell me what was written on the letter?"

At that moment, Allan's heart beat wild.

He was bashful and at the same time enthusiastic, because he wanted to declare himself in a very romantic way. But when he was about to say the first word, he caught sight of Jader and the two friends coming toward them. Allan was not afraid, but he was worried that something might happen to Jessica. She, who was not a fool, observed everything and said, "Allan, how about we go back to your house the other way? There seems to be much faster, and I want to avoid going to meet Jader and his gang. He's an idiot who keeps trying to win me over back in the school with his antics and distasteful jokes. And I also know that he doesn't like you since you always beat him in the championships."

"Okay, let's go," replied Allan.

So, the two quickly left. From time to time, Jessica looked back to make sure the boys didn't follow them. Only when they arrived at the house, with the purchase, did they calm down.

"Wow…Good, you were quick! We are here laughing a lot remembering old cases; certainly, with these cookies and a cup of coffee, now it will get even better," said Mrs. Julia.

Finally, after many conversations, laughter, and that delicious snack, the teacher said goodbye promising that she would come back again. When Telma was leaving through the gate, she said to Allan,

"Have a nice vacation and have a nice trip!"

"Thank you," he replied.

"My friend, Telma, what do you think about Jessica going with my son to my parents' farm? I'm sure she'll have a lot of fun."

Jessica smiled; it seemed that she liked the idea. The same happened with Allan, but the smile ended when Mrs. Telma replied,

"Not this time…I already arranged with some relatives to spend the vacation in a beach house in Santos. But I promise that for the next vacation, we will all go to your parents' farm."

Upon arriving near the car, the two friends took the opportunity to give another hug. It was when Allan approached Jessica and said very quietly, "When we meet again, after the vacation, I promise to tell you what was written in that letter."

Jessica got into the car smiling and said,

"I hope this vacation goes by very quickly!"

The next day, Allan and his parents arrived at Samuel's house early, who was already waiting for them with great anxiety, as he couldn't wait to leave and enjoy the dream farm. Mr. Paulo helped his son carry the luggage to the car, greeted the Smith family, and said to Samuel,

"Behave yourself and be a good boy. Enjoy your holidays!"

"I had promised you this before, Dad," Samuel replied, giving him a hug. Then he got into the car.

"Ok…I'm happy and I hope everything works out. Then, Goodbye!"

Mr. Richard took them to the bus station. When they arrived, they said goodbye briefly, as the bus departure time was approaching. Each of the boys sat by a window. They knew that the trip from Sao Paulo to Minas Gerais was fascinating and did not want to miss anything.

A few minutes later, the bus left. Joy took over Allan and Samuel, who did not miss any details and pointed out everything that caught their attention.

The day was perfect for a trip: the sun reigned absolutely in a beautiful blue sky. Gradually, a cool breeze with the scent of flowers was taking over the environment and beautiful landscapes began to appear enchanting everyone.

At each moment, nature became more fascinating. And when they reached the border of the two states, everyone was speechless in the face of such splendor. They seemed to be seeing a picture painted by the most demanding of artists, and that was…It was a living picture painted by God.

"See, Allan, how high those mountains are…also look at those farms. Each place more beautiful than the other!" Samuel exclaimed, amazed.

Allan, who always liked geography classes, said to his friend,

"Samuel, all that we are seeing, we studied at the school. Notice, there are several coffee farms, others of sugar cane, and some others with animal creations…But what I really like is to see so many virgin forests."

"Yes, Allan, you are right. The best is to be able to observe nature without the influence of man's action. But did you notice that, in certain places that we passed, the vegetation changed its characteristics?"

"Yes, I did. It is because the tropical forest and the cerrado vegetation predominate in this region."

"Wow! I didn't know you were so smart, Allan."

"I really like this subject, but, as our teacher Telma said, we really need to improve in science and history classes."

Allan's mother, who had listened to the two boys' conversation from the beginning, told them,

"I already knew that you are doing poorly in my friend's classes. I would love to help you with something and…Ah! Since we are in Minas Gerais, one of the most important states in Brazil, can you tell me why of this name?"

Allan and Samuel did not want to risk an answer, they were silent and thoughtful. It was then that Mrs. Julia started giving an extra story lesson to the two boys…

"A few years ago, after the discovery of Brazil, Minas Gerais was an unknown region, with many closed forests and only inhabited by the Indians and several wild animals. For years, the Portuguese, who owned the Brazilian territory, had great fear of penetrating those dangerous lands. One day they decided to enter the jungles in search of Indians to enslave them, as they needed labor to work in the fields. With just a few expeditions, they were becoming aware of the wealth existing in the territory. The news that those lands had many gold mines spread quickly and, everywhere, many people began to arrive, who came looking for the so-called and dreamed riches. Full of hope, they crossed rivers, cut down forests, and faced wild animals. Thus, some settlements appeared. In a short time, the region came to be called the 'Territory of Mines' and, later, changed the name to Minas Gerais, because there really was, and still is, a lot of gold, diamonds, and several other precious stones, not counting the infinity of very important ores, including for the world technology…Probably others are yet to be discovered!"

"Wow!" exclaimed Samuel.

"What's it?" Allan asked.

"What an intelligent family, I think that I know nothing."

Everyone laughed at Samuel's funny gist. They soon noticed that the bus had entered a stop, where there were restaurants and stores. Both the driver and the passengers got out to get something to eat. Julia soon paid for a snack, because she knew that the boys must be *starving*.

Samuel, who could not wait to arrive, asked,

"Mrs. Julia, is there a long way to go?"

"No. Soon we will enter the city of Araxa. The farm is close to it. And, as I have already agreed with my brothers, they will be waiting for us to take us."

When they finished their lunch, Allan went into one of the stores to buy some souvenirs, because he really wanted to give gifts to his uncles and grandparents. As soon as he left the store, his mother, who was outside with Samuel, asked him,

"What did you buy, Allan?"

"Look, Mom…I bought this shirt for Grandpa Jorge and this bag for Grandma Maria. For Uncle Alberto, I bought this pocketbook with a pen and this hat…I know he likes it a lot. For Uncle Milton, I bought this lantern; after all, he loves to walk around the farm at night."

"Very well…So let's get on the bus right away because the driver is already calling," Julia said.

The rest of the trip was also super smooth; everyone admired the beautiful nature to the fullest. In the late afternoon, they arrived at the Araxa bus station, and, through the bus window, Allan was soon recognizing his uncles.

"Look, Mom, they came to pick us up by wagon…How cool!"

"Wow! I've never ridden a wagon before," Samuel was all excited.

Allan said goodbye to the driver, grabbed the luggage and immediately ran to meet his uncles. Samuel, who had repeated the same actions, struggled to keep up with his friend.

Allan quickly climbed into the cart, gave his uncles a big hug, and told them,

"This is Samuel, my best friend. I invited him to spend the holidays on the farm, and he will surely love it!"

"It is a great pleasure to have you with us on this vacation and…where is your mother, Allan?" Uncle Milton asked.

"Look. She is coming right there," replied Allan, relieved.

As Julia approached, she was immensely happy to see her brothers again. They had not met for a long time, communicating only by letters. Then she hugged them with tears in her eyes and said,

"What a joy to be here with you; however, last-minute information made me very sad! The guy at the bus station informed me that he no longer had a ticket to Sao Paulo tomorrow morning, just for the night. And Richard is scheduled to travel to London tomorrow at six o'clock. I will have no other option but to get back on this same bus that will be leaving shortly…I wanted to go with you to the farm to hug my mom and dad. Say that I will be back to pick up the boys and then I will spend a weekend with all of you. And…Allan and Samuel, I hope you behave and have judgment. In addition, I wish you a good vacation!"

"Thank you, Mother, and you can be carefree; we will have a lot of judgment. I will tell Grandma and Grandpa; you sent a strong and big hug."

Then Julia said goodbye to everyone gave her son a hug and kisses and got on the bus again.

Minutes later, the four left for the farm. Everyone was comfortable, because the wagon was very spacious and, by the way, very beautiful. Wherever it passed, always attracted everyone's attention, making Uncle Alberto happy and proud. And it was no wonder, at the farm he was the one who cared for it the most, and the horses that led it had a rigorous treatment. On family outings, Uncle Alberto made sure to hold the reins. Since he had light-colored hair and a habit of wearing a hat, he looked very much like an American cowboy.

The boys were very happy; they laughed and talked all the time. Samuel, who had gotten along quickly with his friend's relatives, started calling them uncles too. He told cases with such intimacy that he seemed to have known them for a long time. Not holding so much desire and curiosity, he asked to hold the reins of the wagon a little bit. Uncle Alberto did let him, but he was aware of any possible unforeseen event. Allan soon wanted to do this too, and Uncle Milton laughed heartily at the boys' attitudes and games.

Chapter IV
The Farm

It didn't take long; the wagon was approaching a gate there was the farm. The long-awaited moment for Samuel and Allan, who looked a little tired. Even so, his attention redoubled when Uncle Alberto said:

"We arrived, boys…Allan, tell your friend to keep your eyes wide open, as he will see, perhaps, one of the most beautiful places that exist."

Indeed. The farm, right at the entrance, already gave a preview of being incredible. They entered through the wooden gate and followed a dirt road flanked by trees and shrubs that capriciously stood at the top, thus forming a natural roof. There, through the small cracks, sunlight came in, illuminating the path. Flowers also followed the road until the end. It was possible to catch a glimpse of a huge courtyard where the house was.

Allan was overjoyed to see everything. Soon he saw his grandparents waiting for him on the porch, with open arms. A happy smile appeared on his face and, more than quickly, he got off the wagon in an eagerness to embrace them.

"Grandpa, Grandma, I did miss you," he said. "I couldn't wait to see them again…Here on the farm, everything seems to be as it was before beautiful and peaceful. Run, Samuel, come and meet my grandparents!"

Samuel breathlessly went up the stairs that led to the porch, and Grandpa Jorge immediately asked,

"And this little boy here?"

"This is my friend Samuel, Grandpa. He came to meet you."

"Nice to meet you, Samuel. Feel free and enjoy the delights of our farm. But be careful, because there are dangers here too. Attention should be redoubled in the woods and close to the river."

At this point, Grandma Maria joined the conversation and said,

"What a joy to have you here. The place always comes alive when you come to visit, Allan. And this time it will be even better, with the presence of your friend. It would be complete happiness if your mother was here with us…But, why didn't she come?"

"Oh, Grandma, she had to go back because of my father's travel schedule, but she asked me to give you a hug."

"Yes," said Uncle Alberto approaching. "Julia was very sad but said that when she comes back to pick up the children, she will be here for a few days."

"Come, it's already getting dark. Let's go in, eat something, and get some rest. There will be plenty of time for everything you want to do," Grandpa Jorge said.

Samuel, who was silent all the time listening to everyone, was still impressed by the farm. Then he sighed and exclaimed, "Wow, how many things do I imagine we doing, is not it, Allan? Let's have a lot of fun."

***

The next day, the boys got up very early, euphoric, to see everything and play a lot. They ran to the kitchen and saw Grandpa Jorge and Grandma Maria had already gotten up and prepared a delicious breakfast. The table was full and made them hungry just by looking. Samuel was one who had not seen a table with such variety in a long time: cookies, cake, bread, cornbread, cheese, coffee, milk, juice, sweets, and lots of fruit.

Uncle Milton and Uncle Alberto soon showed up to eat a little; smiling, greeted everyone, sitting at the table.

It was a beautiful day, perfect for the boys to have fun and enjoy every corner of that paradise. From inside the kitchen, you could hear animals in the pasture, the sound of the river, and especially the singing of birds, which looked more like a symphony orchestra, led by the thrush.

Allan, as soon as he finished enjoying his snack, ran quickly to his room and picked up the gifts he had bought on the way. And as soon he entered the kitchen, he said,

"Grandpa, look what I brought…I chose it myself; a shirt and I hope it suits you. And for Grandma, I bought this bag."

"Thanks, Allan, you didn't have to worry. You have already gifted us a lot with your visit, but, anyway, your grandmother and I loved the gifts."

"He's right, my grandson...I loved it so much! You have great taste!" exclaimed Grandma Maria. "But I see that you brought some more things!"

"Yes, Grandma! This one I brought for Uncle Milton. It's a flashlight and I am sure it will help him a lot when he needs to go out at night...And these two are for Uncle Alberto. It's a hat and a pocketbook with a pen."

Allan's uncles were very grateful, as it had been a long time since they received any gifts. Uncle Alberto quickly put on his new hat, looking like a rich farmer, and as soon as he finished eating, he called the boys to go to the corn field. Uncle Milton also went with him; he had a lot to do, as the task of planting and harvesting was entirely his responsibility.

Allan soon realized what his uncle Alberto's intention was and said, "Look, Samuel, look straight ahead. It's a scarecrow, and I bet Uncle's going to put the old hat on him!"

"You got it right, Allan, I will. You remain as smart as ever! But I brought you here for another reason too. We are going to give your uncle Milton a little help in the corn harvest."

"Cool," said Samuel. "I've never participated in a harvest before."

"Glad you liked the idea, Samuel. Tomorrow we will have more services; we will harvest coffee. Know that the farm is not only leisure, but we also must work hard too," Uncle Alberto explained while looking at his own callused hands from working so hard.

Throughout the day, the boys had fun with that new experience of farm workers. They played more than they harvested. The uncles did not demand much from them, they knew they were there to enjoy the holidays, but they wanted to teach them a little bit of everything.

Allan quickly learned the art of corn harvesting and wanting to know more about the farm, asked,

"Uncle Milton. I already know that you are responsible for the plantation...And the other tasks are left to Uncle Alberto?"

"In part, yes! He is responsible for all breeding and takes care of horses, livestock, and all other animals. Your grandfather takes the service of milking the cows, he likes it a lot. And your grandmother takes care of the house. But everyone helps everyone. Today, for example, I needed help with the harvest and my brother came to help me. When he needs help with the animals, I will help him too."

At the end of the day, everyone was very tired, especially Allan and Samuel who were not used to that kind of service.

The next day, Uncle Milton decided to give the boys a break in the coffee harvest. I told them to play a lot, but not to go to the river because it was very dangerous. As soon as they had breakfast, they ran elated toward the pasture; they wanted to see the calf that Uncle Alberto said was born the night before.

"Look, Samuel, there he is! Look, the naughty one doesn't stop breastfeeding; he can barely stand up, but he seems to be very hungry."

"True. And look how many cows and…Wow and that one with an angry face? It must be the father of the calf. See…he looks like a grumpy one. I'm glad we have this fence to protect us."

"Samuel, how about we go to the stable to take care of the horses? Uncle Alberto must be super busy, helping Uncle Milton."

"What a great idea. Cool! But how do you take care of horses?"

"Don't worry, there's no mystery. Come on, I'll teach you."

Allan really had certain knowledge; and it was not for nothing, because, every time he went to the farm, he was watching one of his uncles take care of the creation. He knew that cleaning was essential and, sparing no effort, he started cleaning everything very carefully. Then he changed the water and put hay for the animals to eat.

Samuel was admired with his friend's skill and, fascinated with all that, said,

"I saw that you understand horses, Allan. But would your uncle Alberto let us ride on them?"

"Of course, yes, I don't know if you noticed, but these are the same ones that were pulling the wagon when we were coming to the farm."

"Yes. And?" Samuel was curious.

"Hence, normally all horses that pull a wagon are tame and easy to ride."

"Perfect deduction, Allan. So, let's go find your uncle and ask him."

Uncle Alberto, at first, denied the request but promised that the next day, when all the harvesting work was finished, he would let them ride, but if he went together to give some riding tips.

At night, everyone went to the porch. It was a beautiful night. Samuel was delighted with the sky; it seemed to have more stars and the moon seemed to shine brighter. It was then that something caught his eye and made him scream out of such admiration,

"Look, Allan, a shooting star, how cool! It is so difficult to see these things in the big city, with so many lights around us."

But Allan was not paying attention; he was always like that whenever he heard his grandfather play the viola; even more eating popcorn and drinking delicious orange juice. Sometimes, the noise of some owls interfered with the rhythm of the music, but he didn't even care.

Samuel, who constantly saw something different, kept screaming:

"Look, it's a bat...Look how many fireflies!" And so, the night went by, calm and serene.

***

In the morning, Allan and Samuel woke up super excited. They were dying to ride, but they knew they would have to wait for the uncles to finish harvesting. So, while they waited, they decided to play a lot. They ran back and forth, climbed trees, and swayed on vines crossing from one branch to the other. The excitement was so great that Samuel, delirious with the joke, always said that he was the Tarzan of the jungles. Then they decided to pick fruit. It was such a variety of fruit trees that they were undecided about what to choose.

Finally, Uncle Alberto appeared, he looked tired. With one hand he held the hat and with the other, he wiped the sweat from his face.

"Come on, boys! I promised I would let you ride. I will give some tips and the rest is up to you," said Uncle Alberto, pointing toward the stable.

"That's so cool!" Samuel was excited.

"Attention," Uncle Alberto began his tone firm and sure. "The first tip is essential for a good mount: the horse must feel confident in you. Try to pet it and show a friendly relationship...The second tip is: check if the animal is already tamed and only then put the set of harness parts. The saddle must be securely fastened to prevent a possible fall, and with the reins, you can maneuver it in the desired direction or stop it. Any questions?"

"Nope..."

"How about you, buddy?" Alberto asked Samuel.

"Neither."

"So, good luck to both of you. I would just like to ask you not to go into the closed forest. It is dangerous and it would not be good to come across a jaguar or a poisonous snake. Stay out of trouble," finished Uncle Alberto.

As soon as they prepared the animals, the two boys went out happily riding all over the place. The feeling of freedom was immense, and they were always delirious with all the details that Mother Nature could offer them. After some time, entering trails and trails, the two adventurers approached the banks of the great and famous river. Allan then suggested that they stop for a while so that the horses could rest, and so they would be able to take advantage of that opportunity to stay there, admiring that immensity of water.

Despite its frightening appearance, the river was majestic, beautiful, and fascinating. Its volume of water was very significant and offered a good fishing spot for those who ventured in large or small boats. In the rainy season, it was hardly possible to see the other bank, and few dared to face those dangerous currents. This was the Araguari River, an important tributary of Paranaiba.

Later, when they returned home, Allan saw a small waterfall, inside the forest, that formed from the waters of several streams coming from several springs.

"Look, Samuel, it's a waterfall! To tell you the truth, I had already forgotten about it. It is a perfect place to spend a day of leisure, playing, and relaxing. Notice that the waterfall turned that big stone into a natural pool. We could call Grandma, Grandpa, Uncle Milton, and Uncle Alberto to have a picnic tomorrow, how about that?"

"Great idea, we will definitely have lots of fun!"

"So, as soon as we find the staff, I'll talk about it," finished Allan.

At the end of the afternoon, Allan, taking the moment when everyone was gathered on the porch, savoring a delicious dulce de leche whimsically made by Grandma Maria, did not miss the opportunity to comment on his idea of having a picnic, the next day, at the place where he had seen the waterfall.

At first, everyone was interested and excited; but the next day, it was not so. As soon as the day dawned, Grandma Maria prepared a huge variety of treats: chicken pie, cheese bread, sweets, and juices. She also separated some fruits, medicines, and first-aid utensils. Then she gave Allan and Samuel a hug, telling them,

"Goodbye, have fun, and stay out of trouble! And stay close to Alberto and Milton."

"But why don't you go with us?" Allan asked with a sad look.

"No. Your grandfather is quite down, and I will stay here with him."

"Oh! What a pity. It would be so nice if you and Grandpa went too."

"On another occasion, we will all go together, Allan. I Promise!"

The morning was beautiful, perfect for a picnic and, to improve, all the work on the farm was up to date. Uncle Alberto and Uncle Milton really needed a break, as their tasks were always long and tiring.

Grandma Maria, who had followed all her son's efforts in the past few days, told them, "Life is not just about working! Go and enjoy a lot." Soon after, everyone got on the cart and left toward the waterfall.

On the way, Allan took the opportunity to test his knowledge, wanted to put into practice everything he had learned in his botany classes, identifying each species of native tree or not. His uncles were impressed, as even they, who lived on the farm, sometimes found it difficult to recognize them. Sucupira, Ipe, Angico Vermelho, Jacaranda, and Cedar were some of the important species mentioned by Allan.

Uncle Milton, who was amazed at his nephew's wisdom, said to him, "All right, Allan, keep it up! People never lose by studying and getting information. And since the subject is a tree, do you know the legend of Acaiaca?"

"Acaiaca?!" exclaimed Samuel.

"Yes," stated Uncle Milton. "We know it by the name of Cedar, but the indigenous people in its language call it Acaiaca."

"Then say it already!" said Samuel, all interested.

"Okay, calm down! It is an old legend, but many say it is a true case; so, I'll report in the same way I've always heard. It's like that…

"'The ancient Indians of the region say that many, many years ago there was a supernatural and extraordinary event that would change the life and habits of the entire tribe. That day, everyone celebrated and thanked the god Tupa for the abundance of fish acquired in their fisheries; the children played and ran with the food in their hands, happy to have something to eat. The night was approaching when something very mysterious appeared flying and going toward everyone. It looked like a giant bird, but it was a scary animal never seen by the Indians. Its huge wing was, in fact, extensive leather-like skin that stretched across the entire arm. It had a small tail, a huge comb, and a large beak with several teeth.'

"'The children, in a panic, ran to hide under a tree, huge Cedar and managed to save themselves from the monster's attack. The animal, outraged, landed on one of the branches above. He seemed to want the fish in the hands of the little Indians. The chief of the tribe, terrified by the event, screamed and begged the help of the god Tupa, as his warriors were unable to strike the beast with his arrows.

"Suddenly, a huge and strong light appeared in the sky, which cleared the whole tribe; seconds later, the light soared over the animal, pulling it and making it disappear.

"The children, not to be pulled too, held tightly to the branches of the Cedar and were saved again by the tree. Then the mysterious light disappeared as if it was a lightning bolt in the sky, and the little Indians ran to meet their parents. From that day on, after their fisheries, the whole tribe went to the feet of the sacred Cedar to thank their god for good luck and to ask for protection for the village.'"

"What a strange and exaggerated case, Mr. Milton!" Samuel said with a loud laugh. "Probably, someone who was not very well in his head imagined all this and gradually passed this conversation on…Flying monster, what a nonsense!"

"Well, that's right, that's just an old legend; however, what caught my attention the most is that the person who told it described the animal exactly like a Pterosaur!" deduced Allan.

"Ptero…What?" Samuel asked, all confused.

"Pterosaur, a flying reptile. But it would be impossible, as these animals no longer exist!"

"All right, Allan! Each time I am more surprised with you. Really, the characteristics are really that of a Pterosaur. But, as you said, it would be impossible for such an animal to have appeared near some indigenous tribe, as it was extinct more than 65 million years ago. Except that, inexplicably, strange and very mysterious things have been happening in this region, especially there on that. Well, how about we change the subject? Let's think about having fun," said Uncle Milton, smiling.

"Where Uncle?" Allan asked interested.

"Forget what I said and…See right, there is the waterfall. Until we came fast!" deconstructed the uncle.

"That's cool! I can't wait to play and swim in those waters, I'm so hot," said Samuel happily.

But Allan did not even notice the waterfall, he was silent and could not concentrate on anything else; just find out what mysterious place that his uncle would not tell.

A few minutes later, nature showed its strength and Allan again gave in to the charms of that place. The sound of the waterfall and the song of the birds brought him an enormous feeling of peace and tranquility, making him remember his grandparents, his parents, and Jessica, people whom he really wanted to be there, at that moment.

Samuel barely waited for the cart to stop, jumped out, ran, took a dip, and then shouted at his friend,

"Come, Allan, the water is great!"

"I don't doubt it. I will be leaving shortly, but first I will give my uncles a hand in preparing the picnic."

After everything was ready, Allan and his uncles, not being able to stand the strong sun anymore, dived at once, making a tremendous noise and spreading water everywhere. As well as the heat, the joy and relaxation were also intense, especially in the moments when Samuel invented funny games, animating the environment and making everyone laugh. Finally, after they had a lot of fun, hunger arrived and made everyone stop swimming and run toward those delicacies prepared by Grandma Maria.

"I wish this vacation didn't end anymore," Samuel said, looking at the waterfall. "This place is awesome. Here everything is beautiful and charming; I've never seen such beautiful landscapes and…Hmm, this chicken pie is delicious!"

Later, Uncle Alberto, who was passionate about animals, suggested a walk through the forest, hoping to spot and show the fauna of that place. Everyone really liked the idea and minutes later they were already seeing several animals. Some of them attracted more attention, such as the maned wolf, macaws, toucans, tamarins, and an ocelot, which greatly scared Samuel the moment it passed by them with prey in his mouth. Uncle Milton swore he also saw a jaguar in the distance, but he was unable to show it to the boys, as the damn thing was too fast.

They walked for more than an hour, breaking branches and making paths with machetes. Then they reached the banks of the river, in a place where the boys had not been before. Allan, who loved the adventure, was even more surprised when he spotted on the other side of the river part of huge hills with high Rocky Mountains full of vegetation, which were surrounded by a dense fog, leaving the place with a mysterious and frightening aspect.

"Curious!" exclaimed Allan. "I've never seen these hills before. It is incredible, a place very different from any I have ever seen; it looks like one of those mystical places and it is certainly a full plate for an adventurer."

"I don't want to be that adventurer," then Samuel said, looking at the mountains, a little frightened. "There it should be infested with snakes, lizards, and other poisonous animals. I just don't understand how we didn't see it from the other side of the river!"

"Well, Samuel, in that place, the trees are very tall, and the fog, yesterday, was very low…That must be why we didn't see it! You don't need to worry, we could all go there one of these days, and venture out a lot; how about uncles?"

"No way," said Uncle Milton. "There is no place to play, and if you've never seen her before, it must be because she's like that almost always in the morning, with lots of clouds and a heavy fog…I don't know if you know, Allan, but a lot of that mountain belongs to our farm, but we always avoid going there because it is dangerous and mysterious…Well, let's leave this conversation aside and go home. It's getting too late."

"Oh! Now I know the place that you didn't want to say the other time! It's in the hills. You didn't think I would find out, did you? So, is it in those mountains that weird things are happening?" asked Allan, his eyes shining with joy at having found out.

"You are as smart as you are stubborn. But I already said: we will not go there and…"

Suddenly, a loud roar, resembling that of a huge animal, came from the hills, interrupting Uncle Milton's conversation.

"What's that?" Samuel shouted in alarm.

"Come on, let's go," Uncle Alberto spoke.

"What was that roar, uncles? It didn't sound like a jaguar; it sounded like a much larger animal!"

Allan's uncles did not even answer their nephew's question; they were frightened and walked lightly toward the waterfall. As soon as they arrived, they picked up some things that they left there and soon afterward they all got on the wagon. On the way, Allan, not taking any curiosity, asked again, "What was that, uncles? That roar was anything but ordinary! I am no longer a child…I know you are hiding something. Whether you like it or not, you can see that there is something mysterious there!"

"Okay, Allan. I promise I will tell you everything I know about that place. But be patient, we are all tired and at another time we will talk about it," said Uncle Milton, wiping sweat from his face.

For a few minutes, everyone was silent. In fact, the uncles did not understand why, sometimes, those things happened in that place. To make matters worse, Uncle Milton would try to explain, as he promised his nephew, something that for everyone was inexplicable.

Allan, who was still involved in his thoughts, decided to ask another question on a subject that had been bothering him since the moment he arrived at the farm.

"Uncle, there's something else I would like to know as well…And this I would like you to explain to me now!"

"And what is it, Allan? Your uncle Alberto and I have no intention of hiding anything from you."

"It's about Grandpa Jorge. I have noticed that he has been dejected and discouraged lately. So much so that it was one of the reasons why I came to spend my vacation here because I learned that he is very sad and that, perhaps, he will have to sell the farm."

"Wow, how incredible! In the past vacation, you were just a little boy; today he is an adult, an intelligent, determined boy who cares about family problems. Really, not only your grandfather, but we are all going through difficult times because we will have to make a very important decision and…Damn it! Look who's out there on the porch. If you don't know yet, Allan, that is the number one reason for all our problems."

Chapter V
The Threats

Allan was scared for a few moments, but soon afterward, the sensation he felt was very angry, as he immediately realized that his grandfather was being threatened.

His gaze fixed hard on that tall, rigid man with the white beard and mustache, who was impeccably, dressed in linen pants and jacket, hat, and leather boots. He could clearly see that he wore an eye patch on his face and in one of his hands he held a cigar that he was constantly swallowing, smoking on the balcony.

Allan deduced that he was a powerful person, although he did not seem to him to be a very reliable person.

"Who is that sir, Uncle?"

"It's Colonel Faustino, the devil himself! He's the one who's been taking everyone's sleep here on the farm."

"And those two other men?"

"Iron Fist Tiao and Chico the Ambusher, two dangerous assassins who faithfully obey the colonel's orders. Despicable henchmen, my wish is to…"

"Calm down, Uncle Milton! They are heavily armed." As they got closer to the house, Allan noticed that his grandmother was sitting in a corner of the porch, crying. He quickly jumped out of the cart and ran to hug her, then said loudly to the colonel:

"Listen here, my friend, who are you thinking you are? Can't you see that my grandparents are old people and can't have any major setbacks? Do you think that just because you are an important person you can come here and want to impose something? Leave them alone."

"What an angry boy, Mr. Jorge! Tell him that I just came to talk."

"Talk! Look at my grandmother, see how nervous she is, and she keeps crying."

"I liked you, boy, although you are very cheeky, but I really admire people with a strong personality."

"But I didn't like you not even a little," said Allan.

At that moment, Allan's uncles entered the porch. Uncle Milton couldn't even look at the colonel's face. Uncle Alberto, who at all times tried to remain calm, spoke to his nephew,

"Allan, go to the kitchen and bring your grandmother a glass of water and sugar…And the colonel, do you want to drink something?"

"You don't have to worry. My visit here is quick and to the point. I came to know that your father has decided about what I had proposed to him. I'm an impatient person; I don't like to wait long."

"But you need to be a little more patient. My parents must know what is best for them, after all this is their life."

"I understand, young man, but I am a businessman, and this place is in my plans. I offered you a good sum and it is not the first time I have come here."

"First, what you are offering us is not a good amount! And what we do not understand is your interest in our lands. We know that its strength is cattle breeding, and our farm is small, with little grazing area, not to mention that the colonel already has enough land throughout the region."

"I don't have to satisfy any of my goals and interests. I'm just proposing a deal to you. In fact, this negotiation is going very slow!"

"Okay, Colonel, rest assured that we will resolve this matter as soon as possible."

"Agreed, my fellow Alberto. I will give you a period of three weeks and I hope that by then you will have the definitive answer. One thing I can tell you: you don't want to see me angry; I have a short temper and this place interests me a lot. Am I clear?"

Allan, who had just brought the water to his grandmother, again was not intimidated by the colonel and said,

"They will not sell anything to you!"

"We'll see! Know that my two bodyguards, Tiao and Chico, who are here with me, are very fond of taking my pains and solving my problems in their own way, do you understand?"

"Are you threatening my grandparents? This is a crime, you know?"

"The message has already been given. In three weeks, I will be back. Have a good night!"

Allan, very uncomfortable, barely waited for the colonel to leave and immediately said,

"Grandpa, you can't bow to that man's will. Defend your rights and, if necessary, seek out the regional sheriff and file a threat complaint."

"It is not that simple, my dear grandson. The colonel is very powerful and owns a lot of land. He commands and demands in almost the whole region. The police station itself belongs to him, and the sheriff is nothing but a doormat. Even politicians bow their heads in their presence, as they know who to turn to when it comes to money."

"But there has to be a solution, Grandpa!"

"I see no solution, Allan, the colonel's henchmen are dangerous killers, and it only takes one order for them to come here and finish us off. My family's safety is more important than anything in this life. It is hard to say, but I think I will probably have to sell the farm as soon as possible."

Suddenly, everyone was startled to see Samuel running onto the porch. He was scared and very pale. Sweat ran down his face, and as soon as he took a sip of water, he was able to speak:

"Mr. Jorge, I have very bad news to give you."

"So, speak up, boy. I've had too many annoyances for today. One more or one less won't shake me."

"The thing is, Mr. Jorge. As soon as we arrived from the tour, your son Alberto asked me to take the cart to the stall and let the horses go. But I couldn't do it and decided to come back for help. That was when I saw the colonel and his henchmen whispering and heading toward the car. Immediately, I hid behind a tree, so I could hear perfectly what they were talking about."

"And what was their subject, Samuel? Come on, say it, and spill it!"

"Keep calm, you will need it! It is as follows, I heard the colonel say that tomorrow he will personally look for the owners of the big distributors, warehouses, and stores in the region, to ask that no one buys or negotiates any product from you. He said that he wants to see you in ruin, so you won't be able to deny the sale of the farm."

"Scoundrel…Shameless bandit! I didn't know it was that evil. The proposal he made to me is ridiculous, and if we sell the farm so cheaply, we will have nothing left; we will really be in ruin, begging for help from everyone. We must think and act very quickly because I made a loan at the bank, and I will only be able to repay this commitment with the sale of all coffee and corn we plant. If you want to know, now is war! I will face this demon, from man to man, and I will not think twice before breaking the first one who dares to hurt my family."

"Calm down, Jorge! If God wants, we will find a solution," Grandma Maria tried to calm her husband down.

"Calm is impossible at this point! I will take advantage of the fact that the horses are still in the cart, and I will go right now to look for traders in the region.

"Don't even think about it, Jorge. It is already getting dark, and the road is very dangerous. I know you are anxious, but you will hardly find any open shops at this time."

"You're right, Maria! You're right. There is no point in getting flustered now; tomorrow I will solve everything with patience…At least I hope!"

"Come on, let's go in and get some rest. Surely everyone must be exhausted. But first, let's go to the kitchen where I will prepare delicious chocolate milk," said Grandma Maria, enlivening the environment a little."

***

The next day, Grandpa Jorge didn't even wait for the sun to come up on the horizon to get up and prepare everything. He was determined to go to the nearby towns and urgently find a buyer for his harvest. The prospect of going bankrupt with the colonel's bad intentions was making him very sad and distressed. Then he quickly had his breakfast, accompanied by the boys, who pleaded a lot, the night before, to go too. And, as soon as the star king dawned, they were already sitting in the wagon, anxious and impatient, waiting only for Grandma Maria to give her last recommendations.

"Maria, I don't have all day! Stop treating boys like children. Can't you see they are really grown up? You can rest easy, they will behave very well," said Grandpa Jorge, anxious to leave.

They then finally left. The path felt more like a trail than a road. Despite some small holes, it offered conditions to move. The boys were enjoying the ride, laughing and playing all the time. Sometimes, they remained silent and with their mouths open, admiring with delight the nature, which, so sublime, showed that it was a gift from God.

At a certain point on the road, Allan saw, in the distance, something that not only paralyzed him but accelerated his heart. His attention was completely fixed on the horizon and his face changed as if he were seeing something supernatural. He didn't even blink, because he didn't want to lose sight of the hills, that mysterious place that, surely, hid something. Since when they returned from the picnic, those mountains had not left Allan's head; that horrible noise they heard seemed to be still roaring in their ears. For a moment, he thought of asking his grandfather several questions but saw that he was not in a good moment. One thing was certain: patience and courage were some of his qualities, and it would only be a matter of time. Sooner or later, accompanied or not, he would check and try to unravel that mystery.

After covering a few kilometers, a fact literally put all of Grandpa Jorge's pretensions to the ground. Hidden behind a bush, a huge snake was lurking, ready to strike. The horses, who instinctively understood the situation, ran anxiously to save themselves, causing the wagon to lose control and to fall just ahead, in a sharp curve.

The boys suffered nothing from the impact of the fall. They were very lucky, as they fell on a large thicket of grass. Grandpa Jorge didn't have the same luck and rolled over a ravine that was nearby. From the screams of pain, it was easy to know that he had been hurt badly.

Allan immediately sought to help him; he ran to the edge of the cliff and shouted desperately,

"Grandpa, are you okay?"

"Not so much…Not to mention the bruises and scratches, I think I fractured or sprained my right foot."

"Stay calm! I will think of a way to get you out of there, or I will seek help there."

"Okay, my grandson! I will have patience but try to be quick because it hurts a lot."

Allan soon had an idea. He saw that the only way to pull his grandfather would be with the help of one of the horses. But where would they be? Where would they have fled to? Then he remembered that the wagon, when it fell, remained attached to them and, therefore, they should be close by. Quickly, he asked his friend to stay there and followed the animals. It was not difficult to find them…a few meters away they were calm, taking water in a small stream. In a few minutes, he released one of them, took a rope from the wagon, and returned to the place, convinced that everything would be all right.

When he saw his grandson, Mr. Jorge said smiling,

"Well done, Allan. You did think fast and wisely. You certainly wouldn't be able to pull me, but with the help of the horse, everything will be easier."

"That's right, Grandpa. Now hold the rope tightly and let's get you out of there."

When he saw his grandfather saved from that cliff, Allan thanked God a lot and then suggested that they go look for a doctor, but Grandpa Jorge soon dismissed the idea saying:

"I'm fine, Allan! Do not worry. I thought it was a fracture, but it's just a strong twist that is hurting a lot. Only that is not the problem; what is worrying me is…how will we get back to the site with the wagon tipped over and maybe even broken?"

"Don't worry, Grandpa! I checked and saw that she was almost perfect. What has broken we can easily fix with rope and wood. The most difficult thing will be to unravel it, but in that case, we will use the horse."

"Well done, boy! Each time I am surprised more and more with you. Just…Oh…Hmm. It will be difficult to walk with this painful foot."

"Calm down, Grandpa…Take this tree branch and use it as a crutch. Let's go just before it gets too late."

A few minutes later, the wagon was ready to return. Allan, who at that moment was thinking about all the details, asked his grandfather if he still had any intention of continuing his journey. But he didn't want to, he was all sore and his clothes were torn.

Samuel, who had been very silent with all that fright, started to loosen himself on the way back, using his good humor to brighten up the environment a little. He told several funny cases and even some jokes, but none of that helped to elicit a smile from Grandpa Jorge, who was always sad and very worried. Finally, when he saw that his repertoire of jokes had no effect, he decided to talk seriously and questioned, "But what the hell was that snake? If only I could punch it in the face!"

At that moment, Grandpa Jorge laughed and said,

"Only you yourself to make me laugh, Samuel. But even I am in doubt about that snake. It was all very fast, and it was not possible to identify the species, but, due to how scared the horses were, it must be a jararaca or boa constrictor, because in these regions may appears.”

The matter, which at that moment had become interesting, ended completely when they saw the entrance to the farm. As soon as they entered through the gate, Grandma Maria, who was preparing a delicious orange cake, realized that something had gone wrong. It was impossible for them to arrive so quickly. Immediately put the cake in the oven and went to meet her husband. Upon seeing him in that state, his eyes filled with tears, and, very carefully, helped him down from the cart, telling him,

“Come on, Jorge, let’s go in and take care of those wounds and you don’t even have to tell me that it was Colonel Faustino’s doing.”

“You’re wrong. This time it was not his fault, but another snake.”

Grandma Maria clearly showed in her expression that she did not understand, but she also made no point of understanding. She just tried to concentrate on first aid to her husband, because at that moment it was the most important.

Later, after being medicated, Grandpa Jorge was still in great pain; he walked with great difficulty to sit on one of the chairs on the porch. He was very sad and thoughtful, but he smiled when he saw Allan and Samuel approaching, holding the same plate of cake to offer him. With a loving gesture, he embraced them and said,

“Thank you, boys. This cake must be delicious. Do me one more favor. Bring me my viola, because with it I can forget my hurts.”

Upon receiving the viola, Grandpa Jorge played and sang some songs, but he was totally uninspired. When he saw his wife and children arrive to keep him company, he gave up singing instead and preferred to talk and find a solution to the huge problem he had at hand.

“Glad you arrived. Sit down, I need to talk to you a lot,” Grandpa Jorge spoke with eyes full of tears. “Today I was not happy with my pretensions and everything that happened I don’t even need to say it again. The problem is that our situation has worsened a lot, because, as I was unable to reach the cities, it is obvious that Colonel Faustino will have all the time in the world to force traders to boycott us…It is sad, but I do not see any other solution except to sell the site and pay off debts with creditors.”

“Boycott! But what boys have to do with plantation?” Samuel asked wanting to understand.

Allan, who almost choked on a piece of cake, laughed and explained in detail to his friend,

"Boycott is to cut business relations with someone or any country. Usually, for economic or political reasons, it is a kind of revenge."

"Oh! I thought it was weird, but now I understand."

"I'm the one who doesn't understand, Grandpa! I do not believe that you will give up the game without any resistance…It is certainly what the entire scoundrel wants."

"You're right, Allan," said Uncle Milton in a voice that expressed a lot of anger. "We really can't sit idly waiting for this bastard to take our land. This farm is our life, we depend on it to live, and we will not hand it over like that, easy, to anyone and much less at a bargain price. One thing is certain: we must act and very quickly. Tomorrow Alberto and I will leave our chores and leave early."

"Ah…Now I liked it, Uncle…We must be cunning and intelligent against this scoundrel. Let's show that we are men and that we know how to play better than him!"

"That's right, Allan!" Samuel was all excited. "And tomorrow, don't let me forget my slingshot, which is just in case we run into that damn snake…Let it think of scaring the horses again…I'm going to make a huge bump on that little head!"

"And who said you two are going? This subject is not for children. The situation is getting complicated and dangerous. We must not forget that we are dealing with bad and despicable people…I think it is better, this time, the two of you stay here on the farm, very quiet. I don't want to be worried; after all, you are here to rest and enjoy your vacation."

"Nonsense, Maria, let them go! They just want to stroll and have some fun. Rest assured; nothing will happen. And, as I said before, these two are quite grown up. If it weren't for them, maybe I wouldn't have come out of that hole alive."

"Okay, you can go! But don't mess around. Stay out of trouble and always be close to your uncles, understand? Oh, and if you happen to meet the colonel and his henchmen, I want the four of you to stay away from them! I don't need to worry, do I?"

Milton, Alberto, and Samuel immediately gave thumbs-up, implying that everything going to be alright. However, Allan evaded the question and started to say that he was tired and that he wanted to go to bed right away. In fact, he didn't want to promise something that, perhaps, he couldn't avoid. It would be very difficult to see the colonel and hold on to not, at the very least, kick him in the shin.

Everyone then went to bed waiting for a more peaceful tomorrow.

Chapter VI
Enigmatic Tales

It was enough for the rooster to sing to make Allan jump out of bed and wake up his friend Samuel. In a few minutes, they changed clothes and arranged some things without making a noise. They didn't want to waste time, so they went to the kitchen, reheated the coffee, and got some cookies and cheese. Smartness was with them. After they had eaten, they ran to the coach house leaving the wagon ready to go. It was too early, some stars still insisted on shining in the sky, and only after the last one went out did Uncle Milton and Uncle Alberto appeared at the kitchen door, holding some bags and some papers. Allan just didn't understand the reason for their faces, but he soon called them to get on the cart. And as soon as they approached, they spit on the floor, claiming the coffee was awful.

"Damn, uncles! Reheated coffee is not that bad, it would be bad to find the colonel with his two henchmen."

As soon as they got up, Uncle Alberto took the reins for himself and, with a shout and whip in his hands, put the horses to run. His wagon skills were such that they quickly moved away from the farm.

Despite the beautiful day, everyone was crestfallen and thoughtful. Even the boys were anxious, as they could not wait for everything to be resolved.

The calm was only taking hold of everyone, when the beautiful landscapes began to appear ahead, doing a lot of good to their spirits. And after some time, they were already calm and optimistic, believing more and more that everything would end well.

For everything to end well, it was necessary to arrive at the destination, Samuel knew this perfectly, so much so that he did not detach a single minute from his slingshot, pointing to each bush that came along the way. But this time, luck seemed to be helping; instead of a snake, they were greeted by a beautiful thrush, who presented them with a singing and flying show. The little bird seemed to want to play, it flew over and over the wagon, landing constantly on Uncle Alberto's hat. Sometimes it landed on top of the horses, seeming to look for some insect. Then, as if to say goodbye, he hooted and flew back to the nest. Allan, in an attempt not to lose sight of him, stood up, quickly turning back. Even though the bird was already gone, he kept looking and remained in that position for several minutes. Samuel, intrigued by that, asked his friend to sit down, because something could happen to him, but Allan didn't even pay attention to him, he didn't even seem to have heard a word.

Uncle Milton, who was not a fool, soon understood what was going on and saw that this time he would have to tell, in detail, everything he knew about that place, because the boy, after seeing it, would not take his eyes off a second of those mysterious hills.

It was only when the cart suffered a strong shake, due to some gravels scattered on the road that Allan decided to sit down. For a long time, he was silent, but his curiosity was totally uneasy, begging for information. No longer restraining himself, he looked at the hills and said,

"Uncle Milton…"

"What is it, Allan?" The uncle asked, already half-brooding.

"I know that today is not an ideal day to ask some questions, but I would love to."

"I know what you want to know, Allan! However, to tell you the truth, I don't know that much about those hills; Alberto and I have never been there. The little we know was your grandfather who told us and, coincidentally, he is the only person who went and returned alive from that place…No, I lie…Another person also managed to return, but he did not last long, they found his body already decomposing a few days later…It seems that he was murdered and until today it is not known by whom and why."

"But what a strange thing, I do not understand…It means that, except for Grandpa Jorge and the other who was killed, everyone who went there did not come back? Amazing! How can that be possible? But what were the things Grandpa told you? And how did he get back? And who was this person who was murdered? And. And."

"Calm down, nephew! I'll tell you in detail everything I know. Relax; I won't hide anything from you."

"Sorry, Uncle, I'm just curious!"

"All right. Well, it all started when your grandparents got married and came to this region in search of a more peaceful and promising life. As soon as they arrived, they insistently looked for land to buy that would be good for planting. Despite the difficulties, they were determined to get what they wanted and, after looking so hard, they ended up finding."

"Ah…Good, so that's how the site started?"

"Yes, Allan! Continuing. Your grandfather always tells us that the former owner was a very old man and appeared to be very ill, as he could barely speak and walked with great difficulty, leaning on a cane. The few words he managed to say, with much effort, were that he felt very happy, at that moment, to be negotiating his lands with good people and that he could thus die peacefully with his sister in Rio de Janeiro. With eyes full of tears and a voice that was already hoarse, he added that God had sent them to him and that, certainly, a very important mission was reserved for both or for someone who would come to belong to the family in the future. Later, after everything was resolved, he took his bundle and climbed on the cart. He thought about saying a few more things, but his voice was no longer coming. Then, looking like he didn't want to stop saying, he pointed several times at the hills, also making some signs so that they didn't go to it. Time passed and the farm was getting better and better."

"Each day, a new planting area was prepared, while others, already with their fruits, awaited the right moment for the harvest. All this thanks to his grandfather, who worked hard, day and night, never failing to thank God for the good things in life…Of course, behind a great man, there is always a remarkable woman, and, without a doubt, your grandmother did not escape the rule, because she was very struggling and gifted; I don't know how she managed it, but she found time to take care of the house, us, the breeding and, sometimes, she also helped in the field…It was because her grandparents were so dynamic that one day a fact happened that would take her grandfather to that mountain."

"What fact, Uncle?" Allan asked, his eyes widening.

"It was on your mother's first anniversary. That day, she received several gifts from her godparents, and one of them was very special. As they are refined, fine people who were very concerned about the future, especially of their godchild, that day, in addition to toys, clothes, and sweets, they also included a huge shipment of coffee seedlings. Your grandfather, satisfied, wanted to go and plant right away, but he was shocked when he remembered that there was no more available place on the farm. Then he recalled that part of the hills belonged to his lands and considered that it could be a great option. However, when he recalled the ex-owner's warning, he immediately gave up on the idea. A few days passed and, on a beautiful morning, your grandfather, no longer able to see those coffee seedlings piled up all over the place, decided to return them to his friend Elias, and if, after all, he had explained, he would not accept them back, he would donate to the first besieger he met along the way. When he took the first seedling, his personality as a brave and pioneering man spoke louder; not wanting to waste any more time, he ran to the kitchen and put some food, medicine, and a machete in a bag. Then he went to the living room, knelt in front of a crucifix, and asked God to protect him."

"And Grandma didn't notice anything?"

"No, your grandfather was always very smart and didn't let her notice anything; after all, he didn't want to make her anxious and worried. Surely, if she noticed something, she wouldn't let him go. Anyway…At the end of the prayer, he snuck out without making any noise, hurrying to get to the banks of the river and, when he saw the boat, he pulled it into the water and went down toward the hills."

"Wow, what courage! I would never go to a place like this alone. Especially if someone had warned me not to go. Who knows what or who I could find?" Samuel said.

"Oh…I would go! I would never let fear overcome me and forbid me from going to a place that belonged to me."

Uncle Milton listened patiently to the opinion of the two boys and said, "Allan, each of you two has a side of reason, but it is good to be clear that fear is important in our lives; it is he who inhibits us from many things that, perhaps, could become a tragedy. Your grandfather, for example, almost lost his life in this risky adventure."

"Yes, Uncle, I understand. But what would become of the great discoveries if fear prevented them? What would our country be like if fear had prevented our discoverers from getting here? What would be the first plane flight, if fear had prevented all that? And…"

"Okay, Allan! I have seen that there is no way, you and your grandfather are just the same: stubborn as a mule. What is certain is that, that day, he was very lucky! Or it was his prayers that helped him. He was so anxious to get to the mountain that he did not even remember that a strong storm had fallen the night before, leaving the river very agitated and difficult to navigate. The current of water, on several occasions, almost turned the small boat that, at that moment, appeared to be a toy. The situation was complicated and desperate; the oars did not obey any maneuver; they were there as if they were ornaments. And, when passing through a very rough stretch, the vessel collided violently with a stone, throwing the unconscious at the foot of the hills."

"Poor guy! But how did he get back?"

"Well, Samuel, at first, he saw nothing! He stayed there for a long time and only after he started a light drizzle did, he wake up. As soon as he opened his eyes, he saw that everything was spinning around him; the headache was unbearable, and blood ran down his forehead. He was so groggy that he looked drunk. As he tried to get up, he staggered and fell a few steps forward. Minutes later, yes, he managed to stay upright and see everything around him more clearly. He was very concerned about being there alone, in a totally unknown place. Although he was still a little dizzy, he approached the river and saw his boat shattered, without the slightest condition of repair. At that moment, he regretted very much for being irresponsible and risking his life on a crazy adventure. However, he hardly knew that his problems were just beginning."

"And what else could happen to him?" Samuel asked.

"Everything. Starting with the missing bag of medicine and food, he couldn't even find some fruit to eat. He thought about lighting a fire and getting someone's attention, but with the wood soaked it was impossible. He shouted and called for help several times, but no one could hear him."

"Later, hunger began to tighten, and the survival instinct spoke louder. Then he got up and started looking at those gigantic mountains, noting that the terrain was easy to explore at certain points. However, when he took the first step, he completely froze in panic when he heard several screams around him."

"Wait?! What?! Who was screaming?" Allan was surprised and impressed by the case.

"Hmm. Well, Allan…It's hard to believe, but your grandfather saw several ghostly figures laughing and screaming as if they wanted to frighten him and drive him out."

"Gho…Gho…Ghosts! Lost souls! Oh, my God, let's change the subject soon."

"Samuel, of course, that was not what my uncle meant! Ghosts…that doesn't exist! And besides…"

"It looks like you're the one who didn't understand, Allan! Ghost was exactly what I said! However, 'lost souls', as your friend said, must be the best way to explain those damn apparitions."

"Uncle, you must be kidding!"

"Well, Allan…Whether you believe it or not, that is beside the point. The truth is that, that day, he had terrible and terrifying visions, making him completely static. The only thing he managed to do was stay there, watching those supernatural and hideous figures. Some resembled missing and presumed dead people here in the region."

"Oh my God! Just by hearing this conversation, I'm already scared to death! We better stop."

"Calm down, Samuel, let him finish the story. If you don't want to listen, cover your ears…But then, Uncle? What happened?" Allan asked with interest.

"Well, Allan…At that moment, paralyzed the way he was, the only thing he managed to do was to simulate a faint, staying there quietly with his eyes closed and waiting for that nightmare to end. For a long time, he heard those screams that seemed to have no end. But then, as if by magic, all voices and figures ceased without explanation."

"Strange! Very strange! I can't understand it. After all, what did they want? What reason would there be for that? And what mystery could exist in that place? There must be an explanation for everything. It is a difficult case to believe, but since it is you that is telling me."

"And you still haven't heard anything!" said Uncle Milton, staring at his nephew.

"What? There is more?"

"Yes, your grandfather, realizing that this nightmare was over, snuck up and ran in despair, was going deeper and deeper into the woods of the hills. He was so scared of what he just had seen that he didn't even care which way to go; he just wanted to be far away from the place of those horrible apparitions. At any moment, he watched if something was following him, but, looking back so much, he ended up tripping over a rock that made him fall and roll a few meters ahead. The fall was quite violent; his wounds hurt a lot and were all over his body, however, those pains that seemed unbearable became insignificant in the face of the enormous astonishment that he felt when he saw an open ditch, a few centimeters from him, with two skeletons inside."

"Skeletons!" exclaimed Allan.

"Yes, that's right! Your grandfather told us that, in addition to being small, they had very different skulls from ours. They should probably be from some kind of hominids!"

"Homi…What?!"

"Hominids! From what I remember from our history classes, Samuel, they lived thousands and thousands of years ago. They were beings that looked a little like monkeys but with many human characteristics. What I do not understand is that most of them were from the African continent, and it is unlikely that they had lived here, or rather, there in the hills…Strange!"

"It's very strange, Allan. Inside the pit was a board made of unknown metal, and it contained some information. But there was no way to read it, as it looked like a mixture of ancient Egyptian and Chinese alphabets."

"Egyptian alphabet with Chinese? I huh…I've never heard of any civilization that had such writing!"

"And there isn't, Samuel! The uncle said it just looked. But this is not the most important thing which puzzles me is that everything in that mountain range is mysterious."

"Your grandfather knows that sentiment well, Allan! Frightened by all that, he immediately thought about leaving there and looking for a safe place to try to cross the river. As soon as he turned his back on those bones and started to run, he sensed that something had started to follow him. Terrified, he accelerated as fast as he could and immediately looked for a place to hide. His great experience on the farm made a small cave, surrounded by bushes and trees do not go unnoticed. Of course, there was no need to think twice; in a matter of seconds, he installed himself inside, staying very quiet. Suddenly his heart raced, his ears, which were attentive to any noise, heard footsteps coming towards his hiding place…Seeing that perhaps it would be his end, he chose to go out and face whatever it was. Terrified is the right word to describe his reaction to seeing those skeletons walking and holding stone axes in their hands. It even looked like a nightmare or a horror movie! But it was reality…Those creatures were hunting him as if he were an animal. Lucky or not, a curious fact happened; those dreadful figures did not see him, or else they pretended not to see! They just continued their way as if nothing was happening. So, his grandfather who was not a fool, quickly returned to his shelter and stayed there, asking God that they would not return."

"So, Uncle, did they come back?"

"No."

"And what did he do?"

"Nothing."

"Nothing! What do you mean?"

"Well…When he realized that the sun was setting, he decided not to venture further. To take a risk would be silly because a new surprise could still appear. Therefore, he decided to spend the night there, which was very cold and gloomy. Despite this and the discomfort, he quickly fell into a deep sleep. The next day, already rested, he immediately thought of going ahead to try to get out of those hills. But as soon as he had just woken up, he clearly felt that the ground began to shake and a dense dust, accompanied by a strong odor, began to come from outside. Wanting to go home soon, he decided to go out and start running; however, when he heard a loud roar followed by a roaring noise of trees breaking, he preferred to just look and see what was happening."

"'My God am I dreaming?' were the only words spoken by him at that moment. And it was no wonder, he was so surprised and fearful that he couldn't move any more muscles; he knew he was at high risk of life and any sudden gesture would bring about his end."

"And what was it, Uncle?"

"Calm down, I'll tell you! Well, believe it or not, a huge saber-toothed cat, which looked hungry, cornered a small cub of triceratops, tirelessly threatening it with its huge fangs."

"What?! Saber-toothed cat, triceratops, but…"

"Yeah, that's what you heard, Allan! What's more, the mother, a giant that was about eight meters long, was knocking everything down in front of her to try to save her offspring. The predator, even though it was a notable hunter, realized the graveness of the situation and immediately gave up the onslaught; however, with the hunger it was in, sniffed another prey that, for sure, would be much easier."

"Grandpa!"

"Yes…Bruised and with no weapon to defend himself, it was the right game for that huge animal. So, seeing that the spectator became the meal, he immediately tried to get out of there as soon as possible. He ran so far, aimlessly, and luckily managed to find the river that, he thought, could be his salvation. The problem was how to cross it because the waters were rough, and the current was scary just looking. He knew that any attempt at swimming could also cause him to die. Suddenly, to increase the despair even more, behold the bloody cat roaring and salivating. Its fangs and claws stained with blood from previous victims showed that it was not there to play. And as soon as he frowned, it jumped on its opponent with all his strength and agility. The impact was so great that your grandfather was thrown into the river bleeding and crying in pain."

"Wow, poor guy, but how did he manage to save himself?"

"Good question, Samuel! Well, I think it was a miracle, maybe! I know that, when his forces were ceasing and his hopes were drowning next to him, a huge branch floated by his side; it seemed that it was God's help…I think! In fact, he thought so; too, as soon as he held on, freeing himself from drowning, he looked up at the sky in gratitude and then made the sign of the cross. From then on, everything seemed to be resolved; but it was not like that. The current made the branch look like an insignificant sprig. The danger was imminent; at any moment a waterfall could appear, or he might hit his head violently on a rock. Despite this, he sought to focus only on his prayers; he had faith that his guardian angel was there and would not let anything happen to him…And wasn't he right? Minutes later, the branch caught on a huge rock that gave access to the other bank of the river. Not wanting to miss what, perhaps, could be his only opportunity; he climbed up as quickly as possible and immediately jumped on solid ground, ridding himself of that entire nightmare."

"Phew! What a relief. For a few moments, I thought he wasn't going to come out alive!"

"Now, Samuel, if Grandpa is still alive today, of course he would be fine. What bothers me the most and doesn't come out of my head for a minute are the mysteries that surround the hills…Nothing you did tell us, Uncle, makes sense. It is absurd and difficult to even believe. How can ghosts appear, like this, to others, and even more screaming…Skeletons of hominids chase someone with axes in their hands as if this were a normal thing…And another, a saber-toothed cat, who lived a few thousand years ago attacked a baby dinosaur that was extinct sixty-five million years ago. All of this is completely impossible! There must be an explanation for all this. One thing is certain: that place is a nest of bad eggs."

Uncle Alberto, who had not argued anything since the beginning of the conversation, decided to talk a little about the subject, saying, "You're right, my nephew! Yes, there is a mystery in that place and, really, it is a nest of bad eggs. I say that, because your grandfather never lied to us. Not to mention that we are already tired of hearing screams and roars that come from there; that's scary!"

"Oh! That picnic day, we all heard it. It was a threatening roar," recalled Allan.

"Yes, it's horrible! But thank God, your grandfather managed to return and warned us of the dangers that exist in those hills. I remember it like it was today when I saw him come hurt and crying. I know that we all ran toward him to embrace him; your grandmother, despite the crying, was immensely happy, and only after she thanked God so much for her husband's return, she asked him what had happened. We listened with great attention to everything he reported, and, like any child, we were terrified and perplexed. Several nights we slept, we were afraid to even play outside the house. His grandfather, seeing our dread, gradually reassured us and made us understand that the danger was only in the hills. But, afraid that one day we would decide to venture into those dark mountains, he made us swear on our honor, that we would never go there. And believe it or not, we are honoring our oath to this day."

"Oh! So that's why you haven't been there yet? Well, at least Samuel and I didn't swear anything yet!"

"What? I haven't sworn yet! Oh, my God, so I'll swear now! I will not go to that place, not even dead."

"Stop being silly, Samuel! Have you ever thought about the things we could discover?"

"I don't want to find out anything!"

"Your friend is prudent, Allan. That place is not an amusement park, much less a paradise. If you think about having a long life, get it out of your head…And you think that we would allow it?"

"Okay, Uncle Alberto! You are right…You can rest assured! I swear I will never let my curiosity take me there. Unless one day I need to go."

"Go there for what?"

"Come on, Uncle! It may be that one day someone needs help to get out of there alive."

"Hahahaha…You are too funny, Allan. It seems that one day none of us will be in that hell needing help," Uncle Alberto laughed.

"Yeah, you never know! But does it mean that my mother always knew about that?"

"Yes."

"And why did she never want to tell me?"

"Well…I think she had her reasons and preferred it that way!"

Suddenly, a muffled snore caught everyone's attention there and caused the controversial issue of those hills to end. Samuel, more than embarrassed, asked them:

"Gosh, what a thing…Did you hear that? I think it was my belly! This whole story made me hungry and…What do we have there to eat?"

Uncle Alberto, again, laughed and told them,

"Inside the bags, we have sandwiches, fruits, cookies, and juice. I will stop the cart in that shade, and we will all eat and rest for a while."

"Yay! That's good!" exclaimed Allan, his eyes widening at the bag. "I must admit that reheated coffee, it wasn't really that great! Come on, Samuel, I'm going to show you how to make a triple sandwich."

Thanks to that delicious bag of treats and the enormous hunger of the boys, the case of the mysterious hills was finally forgotten for a while. However, Uncle Milton and Uncle Alberto looked at each other suspiciously, fearing that their nephew could, at any moment, resume that inconvenient conversation.

Chapter VII
Frustrations

Finally, after almost an hour from the place where they had their lunch, they approached the first city. For a moment, everyone was silent and apprehensive, for they feared that pest Colonel Faustino had already passed by, imposing his will.

Allan, seeing his uncles' nervousness and anxiety, told them,

"I once heard my father say to one of his friends that optimism is fundamental in all the pretensions of a trader. And to be successful in a negotiation, it is also essential to have a good conversation, unbeatable prices, and strong arguments."

"Your father is quite right, nephew."

"I pay close attention to everything he says, Uncle Milton, and I really want to help solve this problem!"

"Oh! I know! But where and with whom are we going to start arguing something?" Samuel asked interestedly.

"Well, I think I brought noted some names and addresses of people we should look for…If I'm not mistaken, the notes are in the bag!"

"Are these, Mr. Milton?"

"Yes, absolutely, Samuel. Thank you!"

"Look at the movement of that street! There are several trades!" said Allan.

"Wow! How this city has grown! There was almost nothing here recently…And if I'm not mistaken, this is the street we should go to…What's its name?"

"Well, from what is written on that board, Uncle, it's…Baron…Baron of coffee."

"Let's see what it says on the note. Hmm, this is the street! Alberto, stop there, and let's get down to business, and boys, take care of the cart."

"Ah…" they complained together.

"I told you, stay here!"

Later, Allan, already impatient with his uncles' delay, decided to go after it and see what was going on. His desire was to be with them and help them.

As soon as he started walking down the street, a conversation by some gentlemen who were passing by attracted his attention, as it was a subject that interested him. Allan returned and said to his friend, "Samuel, those men are saying something about Colonel Faustino! Stay here…I'll follow them and try to hear a little more about what they're talking about! Okay?"

"Yes! But come back soon. I don't want to be here alone for too long. You know what; I'm already getting scared of this whole story. And I think…"

Allan barely let his friend complete the sentence; he ran very fast and stayed close to those people, pretending to be playing.

And as soon as they stopped in a small square, he sat on a bench and stood there listening to everything.

"Samuel!" shouted Alberto.

"Oh my God, you scared me! I'm glad you guys arrived."

"Where is Allan?" The uncles asked together.

"Oh! He left me here talking to myself and ran after some men to listen to what they were talking…"

"Talking? But talking about what? And who are these men?" Uncle Milton asked, already nervous.

"I don't know. Some gentlemen came by saying something about Colonel Faustino."

"I knew it! That is why we have achieved nothing in this 'blessed city!' Surely this has the finger of that pest…Damn you!" said Uncle Alberto, irritated.

"So, let's go. I'm worried about Allan. Did you see which way he went, Samuel?"

"Yes, Mr. Milton. He went to that square."

"Stubborn boy! I asked you both to stay here. The problems we have are enough already and the last thing we need is for him to go missing."

"You can stop worrying, Mr. Milton. Here he comes, look and…Wow! Apparently, he doesn't bring good news."

"Uncles. Sorry for getting away from here! But I had to follow a few gentlemen who have just said something about the colonel."

"Your friend told us, Allan…So, what did you hear?" Uncle Alberto asked.

"What you feared! He managed to get here before us, and the worst thing, he has already skyrocketed toward other cities."

"Damn snake!" shouted Uncle Alberto.

"And there's more! He put his two faithful henchmen to help with the mission. From what I heard; each took a different course to save time."

"Bastard, and now, Milton, what are we going to do?"

"Calm down, Alberto, now we can only count on luck." Much later, after visiting almost all the villages, Allan and his uncles concluded that luck was not even close to them. No one until that moment had been interested in or dared to negotiate with them. Nervous and upset, they thought of returning; but, when they saw large black clouds gathering in the sky and the night approaching, they immediately gave up on that idea.

Uncle Alberto, concerned with the boys and with the tiredness of the horses, suggested that they spend the night in a small town a kilometer from where they were. As soon as they arrived, they immediately looked for a pension and then went to sleep.

***

The next day, they got up very early, had a hearty breakfast, and left. Uncle Milton and Uncle Alberto went alone to some establishments. They seemed very discouraged and, always, showed signs of exhaustion and a great desire to return home. The boys, on the contrary, seemed in a good mood, as they wanted to play and were in no hurry to leave. When they realized that the sun was shining brightly, they entered a small stream and, after swimming a lot, decided to climb on a mango tree to get some fruit. Suddenly, Allan, who was already at a good height, almost fell from the tree, after getting scared. Intrigued by that, Samuel asked:

"What is it, Allan? Say it!"

"Look over there, near the stream. It is Colonel Faustino and his henchmen…Bastards! I bet they already have done the dirty work!"

"For sure, Allan! So, what are we going to do?"

"Oh, I do not know. My wish is to go there and punch them…"

"Oh, I know! Samuel, can I borrow your slingshot?"

"What will you do?"

"You will see!"

"No, I don't want to see!"

Allan quickly descended from the tree, picked up a mango seed, and, with the precision of making any sniper envious, hit the colonel in the back of the neck, making him fall into the creek. His henchmen, who understood nothing and tried their best not to laugh, immediately jumped into the water and lifted the powerful boss with the greatest care.

"My God! You're nuts! Let's run," said Samuel worriedly.

"Easy, they didn't see us. But to be sure, let's go back down that trail."

"Oh my God! Look, Allan, there's an Indian sitting under that tree!"

"It's all right! He's just an Indian…And he looks a little old."

"Yes, I realized! As soon as we get past him, we will show our education and greet him!" said Samuel.

"Hello, how are you, is everything okay?" Allan asked, smiling.

"Yes! Or rather…More or less, but never mind! If I may, I would like to tell you to beware of those men. An hour ago, I was there in the square, selling some handicrafts, when I heard them threatening several people."

"We already know that! They are trying to harm my grandfather…I hate them!"

"You are a brave boy. I saw what you did, and I was amazed by your aim. You remember me a lot of my son…Too bad, he's not with me anymore."

"He's not? And that is because?" Samuel asked, all interested.

"Well, that is a long story. In fact, I don't like to remember the day he disappeared. Uirapuru was a good son! Intelligent, brave, and very close to everyone in the village. A little warrior who was preparing to be the future chief of the tribe. Today, if he is alive, he is about your age."

"Uirapuru! That is a bird's name, isn't it?" Allan asked.

"Yes! A beautiful medium-sized bird whose song, although rare to be heard, is very pleasant," explained the wise Indian.

"Well, I'm sorry for your son's disappearance…Sir?…"

"Acaua! In the language of my tribe, it means 'great bird that hunts snakes'…And you, what are you called?"

"My name is Allan Smith, and this is my friend, Samuel. I would like to ask you just one more thing…Do you have no clue as to where your son may be?"

"The day he disappeared, I was ill; I felt severe pain all over my body and a lot of indisposition to go hunting. Seeing my dismay, he came and asked me if he could go in my place; only then would he put into practice everything he had learned with the bow and the arrow, showing everyone that he was already a man. Without any fear, I authorized it. I knew that he knew the forest well and that this was his big chance to show that he was capable. I just recommended that you pay close attention, as Mother Nature does not forgive the weak and inattentive…He quickly painted his face, asked the God Tupa for protection, and left the village with firm steps. After that day, I never saw him again, and that has been over two years. In the first days, we looked for the entire forest to discover any trace that could solve the mystery of its disappearance; but it was all in vain! All I know is that I miss him so much and one day I dream of finding him. That's why I never stopped leaving the village. Today, I sell my handicrafts, as it helps to distract me and renews my hopes of finding him in some village."

"Clue, you said you didn't find it, but do you have any suspicion of where Uirapuru might be?" Allan continued to ask.

"Hmm! Yes, I have," replied the old Indian, with a trembling voice and an expression of panic.

"But what are you waiting for to go there?" Samuel asked, puzzled.

"It is a forbidden place for my entire tribe. It is an extremely dangerous region and…"

"And what? Continue, Mr. Acaua!" Samuel insisted, his eyes wide.

"Haunted," completed the old Indian.

"Haunted! Are you sure?" Allan was also interested.

"Yes…Weird things happen in those lands. Gigantic beasts appear out of nowhere…And evil spirits roam all day."

"Oh my God! You better keep looking for your son somewhere else!" said Samuel, completely terrified.

"Is the place you are referring to hills a few kilometers from here?"

"Yes, Allan! Do you know it?"

"No! Only my grandfather! As far as I know, he managed to escape by sheer luck and never dared to return! And well a part of that area belongs to him and, even so, he forbade the whole family to go there."

"And he did very well because what I know is that almost no one returns alive. I would even like to meet your grandfather!"

"Glad to!" exclaimed Allan. "And what else do you know about that place?"

"Well, since I was a child, I heard the elders of the tribe saying horrors of those damn hills…They talked about the screams and roars of gigantic monsters. Sometimes, some warriors and I have even witnessed spirits floating on the banks of the river and, since then, we have avoided even looking in that direction. I remember when…"

"Is your village very close to the mountains?" Samuel interrupted.

"Yes. That is why we have cases and cases to tell…But nothing compares to what I witnessed one day…Once, my village was celebrating, an abundant fishery. At dusk, a mysterious animal flew over us all. That creature seemed to want the fish in our hands. To protect ourselves, we ran under an Acaiaca and."

"Yes, we already know that legend! My uncle told us."

"But this is not a legend; I am one of those children! And I remember very well where that mysterious animal came from…It was from the hills!"

"Gosh, my uncles need to know that!" said Allan euphorically.

"I hope you understand why I still haven't gone after my son in that region."

"Yes…I mean. I, perhaps, would take the risk to save a son or any other relative."

"I really admire your courage and sincerity, Allan! Sometimes, I think like you; but I'm not sure he can be there. He knew that the place was forbidden. My biggest fear is to die in vain and not find him…Another thing that prevents me is that I have two young daughters who depend on me; Irani and Jaci, very beautiful identical twins, who resemble my late wife so much. I hope that one day I can see them married and thus have several grandchildren."

"Now I understand you better. Well, all this talking is good, but we must go. My uncles must be waiting for us."

"I'll go with you! I want to show you the path and protect you from these bandits."

"Thank you, Mr. Acaua! So, let's go; but I want to make it very clear that I am not afraid of any of these idiots. One day they will regret everything they are doing to my grandfather.

The three of them quickly arrived near the pension's entrance, where they settled in the last night, and there were already the uncles with sad, downcast eyes and not wanting to say anything more about the negotiations. They just asked where the boys were and who was the new friend with beautiful macaw feathers on their heads and a big bow hanging from their backs.

"This is Mr. Acaua, uncles. We met just now, there; very close to the stream…He is a good guy and is looking for his son, who disappeared some time ago."

"Apparently, you speak Portuguese?" Uncle Milton asked.

"Yes! I learned very early, even when I was young. Before, I only spoke Tupi Guarani and had a hard time communicating with white men during the sale of handicrafts. So, I tried to learn the Portuguese language as quickly as possible and today, thanks to me, everyone from my tribe speaks fluently…"

"Yeah…I only know one thing, Alberto and I, not even speaking good Portuguese, we managed to negotiate anything anywhere."

"Don't be sad, my good friend! What's your name again?" The old Indian asked.

"Milton. And this is my brother Alberto."

"Nice to meet you. As the boys already said, my name is Acaua…I would like to tell you something: you are not achieving success in business because of the evil men."

"Apparently, you're already aware of what is happening! And you don't even have to tell me that you saw them," replied Uncle Alberto.

"Yes! Sometimes. But the best time was when your nephew hit the older man with a mango seed and threw him into the stream…"

"What! Did you do that, Allan?"

"Sorry, Uncle Milton! I couldn't control myself."

"No need to apologize. That dog deserved it so much more!"

"Would have been good if he had drowned."

"Enough talk, and let's go. We have a long way back to the farm." Uncle Alberto was worried about the time, as it was getting dark.

"Goodbye, Mister Acaua! It was a pleasure to meet you," said Samuel.

"The pleasure was all mine. It is not every day that we meet special people, just like you!"

"Will you continue here in the city?" Allan asked.

"No! I've sold enough and I intend to go back to my tribe."

"That's cool! Then you can go with us! From what you told us, your village is very close to our farm. The good thing is that on the way you will be able to tell my uncles everything you know about those hills and the legend of Acaiaca…Which is no legend!"

"I'd love to, Allan! If your uncles agree with that."

"But of course, it will be a pleasure; even more, since you are from the tribe that is close to our land, and which is very well-spoken!"

"Thank you, Mr. Milton! I'm happy for the compliment!"

"The wagon is right there…And, for sure, we would love to hear everything you know about that mountain and this legend that, to tell you the truth, my brother and I already suspected that it was not a simple 'little story', but, yes, a fact! Ah…And before I forget, tell us, too, everything you know about your son's disappearance; this if it is no hassle!"

"Yes, I will, Mr. Alberto. The trip is long, and we will have a lot to talk about."

Chapter VIII
Colonel's Interests

In the late afternoon, the wagon approached the farm gate. They were all tired, hungry, and crazy for a bath. Samuel went down quickly, opened the gate, and waited for everyone to enter. The old Indian, dying of homesickness and seeing that it was late, decided not to enter; but he promised that he would return with his daughters to pay a visit.

Uncle Alberto, seeing that the poor Indian was perhaps hungry, picked some fruit, right there near the gate, and offered it to his new friend, saying, "Do not take too long to visit us, Mr. Acaua. I'm sure you will like my parents a lot…From now on, we will all be on the lookout for some clue from your son."

"Thank you!" he thanked the old Indian, saying goodbye to everyone.

Allan, who had been very fond of the indigenous man, watched him leave and wished with all his heart that one day someone could find little Uirapuru alive. Then he ran toward the house, shouting, "Grandma, Grandpa…We're back!"

Grandma Maria soon opened the door to the living room, and, with a smile on her face, she thanked God that nothing bad had happened. Then she embraced them, affectionately, saying, "Come on, let's go in! Jorge is there at the wood stove cooking a meat with vegetables."

"Apparently, Grandma, he's already getting better from his injuries! I'm going to talk with him…"

"I'm going too!" said the friend.

"Grandpa, but what is this good smell?"

"Ah…This is a family secret…But you really want to know? The best seasoning is hunger! So, how were the negotiations and the trip?" Grandpa Jorge asked, looking seriously at the boys and then at the children.

"Hmm! The trip was smooth, Grandpa…But the rest did not go very well. I prefer that Uncle Milton and Uncle Alberto explain what happened."

"I already expected," Grandpa Jorge spoke very sad and crestfallen. "Well, let's do the following, you are going to take a nice shower, while I stir the pans here…Later we talk, right?"

That evening, after a delicious and hearty dinner, everyone gathered on the porch for that inevitable conversation. Clearly, everyone's face of sadness was visible, especially that of the head of the family.

The moment was of such concern because they would have to sell, quickly, everything they planted, or they would be left with a heavy bank debt.

Samuel, seeing everyone's dejection, immediately thought about relaxing the environment a little. He then started by telling the funny and interesting facts that happened along the way. He detailed everything very clearly and tried to praise the new friend of the family. Only in a moment, so Allan would not get into trouble with his grandfather, did he lie when he said that the colonel fell into the stream for slipping on a spoiled fruit.

"Spoiled, I wish it were his face!" Grandpa Jorge commented angrily. "Now, in relation to our new friend, Mr. Acaua, I hope he will visit us very quickly, because, as things are going, soon we will no longer have the farm."

"Don't say that, Jorge. If God wants, we will find a solution," Grandma Maria had tears in her eyes when she spoke.

"Grandpa, I had an idea! Since you have achieved nothing here in these regions, why don't you try there in Araxa, or, in the last case, Belo Horizonte, which is one of the largest cities in Brazil?"

"Good thinking, Allan! If Milton agrees, tomorrow…"

"Yes, I agree, Alberto! But let's leave it for the day after tomorrow, because I would like to update some things here on the site, agreed?"

"Deal," replied the brother.

"I would just like to remind you that, if we manage to negotiate something, our profit will be much less. It is obvious that we will have very high expenses with transport and freight."

"It doesn't matter, Uncle! What matters is Grandpa paying off the bank loan right away. And this time, without the colonel's meddling, you'll make it."

"Yay! Let's get to know Araxa and Belo Horizonte. That's cool!"

"Don't get me wrong, Samuel, but I think that this time is better you and Allan stay around enjoying the holidays. These cities are quite large, and it is good to avoid any kind of problem!"

"Okay, Mr. Milton!"

"Well, let's go to sleep," Grandma Maria ended, yawning with sleep.

***

The next day, everyone got up very early and excited. And as soon as they ate tasty cornmeal bread accompanied by a delicious coffee with milk, Uncle Milton, Uncle Alberto, and Grandpa Jorge went out to take care of the animals and collect some wood for the stove. The boys, this time, seeing that Grandma Maria seemed a little sad, preferred to give her a little help with the housework. Only later, after they had lunch and cleaned everything, did they decide to go out to play.

Unlike Allan, his friend was crazy to have fun. It wasn't every day of the year that you were privileged to be on a wonderful farm like that. Although they were the same age, it was clear that Samuel was much more of a child; as soon as he left home, he started to run, everywhere, scaring the hens and laughing out loud at seeing them, desperate, disappearing into the bush. Soon after, he jumped over the corral fence, made faces at the cows, and when he realized that some were coming toward him, he jumped back, laughing. Then he challenged his friend to a test, where they would have to run and climb a huge avocado tree that was about thirty meters from where they were. It was the only moment when he didn't laugh, as he slipped in the mud, lost the race, and got his face all dirty with clay.

From the top of the tree, Allan spotted the mysterious hills and, for a few seconds, was static and thoughtful.

"Samuel, I had an idea! What do you think if we go…?"

"No way! In those mountains, I would not go even if someone paid me! I'm afraid to even look at them."

"That's not where I'm thinking of going today! Although one day I will…"

"My God! And where do you want to go? Go on, say it!"

"There on Colonel Faustino's farm."

"What! You are completely crazy. I'll not…"

"But not even for a good cause?"

"Hmm! I don't know! But tell me, what are you up to?"

"Well, I was thinking that we could go there quickly, sneak in, and try to hear something."

"But to hear what? Dammit."

"Hey, Samuel! What world are you in? Wake up!"

"Oh! I get it! Now I understand. You want to know what his interest is in buying the farm, don't you?"

"Yes…Interest not only for the farm but for the hills and its mysteries. It is always good to remember that a large part of those mountains belongs to Grandpa Jorge, and no one will get it out of my head that the colonel knows something about it."

"You're right! Want to go, and then let's go! Just give me a few minutes to change clothes, wash my face, and pick up a few things."

Half an hour later, Samuel came clean, hair combed and with a bag in his hand.

"What are you taking with you, Samuel?"

"Just a few little things! I don't know if your uncles will care, but I decided to borrow some of the gifts you gave them."

"Yes, but for what?" Allan asked, very curious.

"Well, I think it will be very useful to take the pocketbook with a pen, in case we need to write down something important…I also took some fruits and the flashlight, in case it gets dark…What do you think?"

"Very well, partner! Let's go."

"Just a little question…Will we go on foot or in the wagon?"

"Samuel, I don't want my relatives to know where we're going. Certainly, they will not let us go if they hear about our plans…We will leave very discreet, walking there. Rest assured, the colonel's farm is one and a half kilometers east of here. There's no way we will get it wrong. We can follow the road or go along the river…You decide!"

"All right. So, let's go on the road, which I'm a little afraid of the river. And, after all, how do you know when it is north, south, east, and west?"

"It's very simple, Samuel! Come, on the way, I'll explain."

Allan, who was anything but silly, asked his friend to run for time. He really wanted to be brief, he was worried and didn't want to come back late. At first, they were going fast, but when he realized that he couldn't memorize what he had learned, Samuel started to stop, all the time, to remember and ask,

"How was it? Right hand, I point to the east, where the sun rises; left hand to the west; in front of me is the north and behind the south…I don't think I forget anymore!"

After several stops, pointing their hands back and forth, they finally managed to spot the farm and, quickly, hid behind a bush near the gate, staying there for a few minutes watching.

"So, Allan…Do you see the colonel?"

"No…Neither he nor his two watchdogs!"

"Watchdogs? Oh, my God, you didn't tell me anything about dogs!"

"I didn't say dogs, Samuel! I'm talking about the two henchmen."

"Oh…I get it! So, aren't we going in?"

"Calm down, be patient. Haste makes waste. We must make sure that we are not being seen! Look up there, on that hill! There are some people working in the fields. And there in the corral is a man putting water for the cows."

"Wow, I hadn't even seen it! But will we have to wait for all these cows to drink water there!"

"Well, I don't think so! But look, he just left and is heading toward the pasture."

"So, let's go because the others who were in the field also disappeared from the view!"

"Wait, Samuel! Stay down and be silent! Look who just arrived."

"Who, Allan? Oh…Gosh, God help me!"

"The scoundrels are returning today! Look at the trunk of the car, it's full of bags and even has a suitcase…Surely, they must have stayed in that small town where Mr. Acaua was."

"It's very likely!"

"Pay attention, Samuel…As soon as they enter, we will hide in the middle of those plants, near the windows, understand?"

"Yes!"

During the time that the boys stayed there, waiting for the right moment to act, they reflected a lot on the high risk they ran. They would have to be astute and cold-blooded to avoid being discovered by those dangerous killers. Any hesitation could be the end for them, regardless of whether they are children.

Despite all that tension, the boys had already decided that they would face that nightmare. And, as soon as the scoundrels entered the mansion, Allan got up and ran like never before, heading toward one of the windows, which was half-open. Then he hid among the plants and gave a thumbs-up.

Samuel, who quickly understood that gesture, also created courage, and as soon as he approached, he took two pens out of the bag and the pocketbook, saying very quietly,

"Take this sheet of paper that I pulled out…We both better take notes on things that might be important!"

"Good point, partner!"

From where the boys were, you could hear almost everything that came from inside. The problem was that the colonel was talking from one room to another. Then, more than quickly, Samuel crawled to hide next to another window. He knew it was closed, but anything he could hear would help a lot.

The conversation between the trio was unimportant. They remembered and laughed at the events they witnessed in the countless small towns in which they passed and at the panic that merchants felt when they were threatened.

Allan, who could no longer bear to hear so much useless talking, was eager to hear and write down anything that would help his grandfather. Impatient, he began to be saddened, thinking he would leave without any important information. But that was his lucky day, and just when he thought to ask his friend to leave, he heard the colonel say,

"I hope, my faithful companions that our efforts will bring about the result that I hope for. Now we just must be patient and wait for the whole plantation of that stubborn Mr. Jorge to rot. The poor guy will surely come to me crazy to sell his land at a bargain price…And the good thing is that he and his two country kids don't even imagine that they are worth a fortune."

"You are very smart, boss," said Iron Fist Tiao. "It was very good for us to know what that geologist discovered in those mountains."

"Certainly, Tiao! I remember perfectly the day he came here. It looks like it was until yesterday! I know it was raining and it was getting dark. The guy came running like crazy, he was all wet and with several injuries on his body. The interesting thing is that he was saying crazy things…"

"I think he was crazy, boss! The boy must have hit his head on one of those rocks and, for sure, he went crazy. You remember that he kept saying that he was chased down in the hills by dinosaurs; by ghosts and that his two companions were devoured by a huge tiger. Crazy!"

"I have my doubts!" commented Chico the Ambusher.

"It may be that the poor guy spoke the truth! When I was a child, my dear father, May God have mercy on his soul, worked on a farm near an indigenous tribe. I remember some Indians who sometimes came over there to ask for some milk and sugar…One day they commented that the hills were haunted and that spirits wandered terrifying everyone. They also talked about giant animals that ate people and…"

"Stop being silly, Chico! Tiao is right. The guy must have slipped, hit his head and went a little crazy…The other two, perhaps, did not have the same 'luck' and died there. What matters is that one of the things he said was true. They were employees of the Federal Government. Your documents and reports prove everything, and the best thing is that only we know about the discovery."

"I know is that the poor guy agonized long before he died, boss," said Chico the Ambusher, looking at his knife. "As soon as you ordered, I stabbed him in the back three times, and then, seeing that he never died, I cut his neck and threw the body into the river."

"You did a nice job, Chico! You two will be well rewarded soon, very soon."

"Thank you, boss! Just to remember, what is called the mineral that the geologist discovered?"

"I'll tell you soon! Come on, let's go to the other room where I will read this report for you."

At that moment, Allan was disoriented. Then, more than quickly, he waved and gestured to his friend, alerting him to be attentive in the conversation. Samuel, without ceremony, stuck his ear to the window and managed to hear, at least a little, what Colonel Faustino was reading.

"The National Research Council, sponsored by the Federal Government, aims to discover and study our mineral wealth throughout the Brazilian territory."

"Here it clearly says that: A mineral containing a high content of uranium was discovered in some parts of the mountain."

"But what is this uranium for, boss?"

Tiao asked, interested.

"Well, from what it says: 'It is mainly used in the construction of atomic bombs and, in the future, for obtaining electrical energy,' it also says here that: The largest discovered deposit is located exactly in the region that belongs to Mr. Jorge."

"But what does the boss intend to do with this discovery?" Chico asked.

"Well, if I get that imbecile's land, I'll sell it for a fortune to the Americans or the Russians. These two nations are certainly the most interested in this rich source of energy."

Without wasting much time, Samuel wrote down everything he had just heard; then he made a positive sign, indicating that they could already leave.

At that moment, Allan noticed that the young man, who a few minutes ago was giving water to the cows, was returning from the pasture. Worried that they might be discovered, he spoke very quietly to his friend, "Get down and stay hidden!"

Samuel, when he saw the cowboy approaching the corral, knelt behind the plants and began to pray. His panic was so great that he got up and ran in despair saying,

"Run! He must have seen us and is going to call the colonel."

Allan, having no other way, ran more than quickly and went through the woods, after his friend. The man, who until then had not seen them, noticed that rush and immediately went to warn the boss.

When they were well away and out of danger, the boys decided to stop for a while and rest under a tree.

"Allan, we ran so fast that we are almost there…Take some fruit out of the bag, you must be hungry!"

"Yeah! I'm hungry. Thank you!"

"You know what; I'm very ashamed of my attitude of running like crazy!"

"You needn't be ashamed, Samuel! I admired your courage, from the moment you agreed to go with me on that scoundrel's farm."

"Seriously?"

"Yes! And I say more, I am very proud to have a friend, like you…"

"Wow, that's cool! I never heard that from anyone."

"Believe me! But, changing the subject, I can't wait to arrive and tell everything we heard to Grandpa."

"Me too!"

"But so…What did you hear from that scoundrel?"

"A very important thing, Allan! It's a good thing I wrote everything down here in the pocketbook. Just a minute, I'll get it and…Oh, my God, where is it? This is all I need; I lost the pocketbook, what now?"

"Lost, are you sure?"

"I think so. I put it here in this pocket and it must have fallen by the time I got up to run. Oh, my God, I can't believe it! Will we have to go back to find it?"

"This is crazy, Samuel! We've been too lucky today and we shouldn't take any chances. The way is to pray and hope that she has fallen somewhere else."

"I...I don't know! I think I lost it right there."

"It's all right. So, let's think like this: If they happen to find it, they will have no way of knowing that it was us."

"Yeah, it could be...The luck is that my letters came out horrible and some words I wrote in half. But even so, they can be suspicious!"

"You're right, Samuel! But don't worry; tomorrow, if you like, we'll be back very early to try to find it. And it's worth remembering that it was a gift for Uncle Alberto."

"Wow, I'm so embarrassed!"

"Don't be silly. The important now is to know if you remember the things you heard."

"Yes, I remember everything! Do you know that geologist? He discovered Uranus various points in the mountains."

"Uranus, Samuel! Uranus is a planet. Did you mean uranium?"

"Yes, that...And the most important thing is that the largest deposit is right in the mountains of the farm."

"Hmm. Now I understand everything! Or rather, almost everything! Come on Samuel, it's time to rest and the staff must be worried...I'm glad you remembered to bring the flashlight, the hours passed quickly, and soon it will get dark."

***

At that same moment, Colonel Faustino, who had already been warned of the two boys who invaded his farm, was carefully analyzing that pocketbook delivered, also, by the cowboy.

"My goodness, what a horrible handwriting! I don't understand anything. I think that sometimes this eye patch makes it difficult for me to read...It seems that the words are half done!"

80

"It's not the eye patch, boss, he wrote almost everything in half! The only things I'm able to read there are: Deposit, farm, Uranus or uranium, we can't really understand…"

"Are you sure, Chico?"

"Yes, boss!"

"Hmm. What the hell! Who are these brats, what were they doing here and with what intention did they write these things down?"

"Don't worry, boss! It must be one of those kids here in the region that came in to steal some fruit and accidentally heard something from our prose."

"I don't know, Chico! Something tells me that one of those kids is that cheeky grandson of Mr. Jorge."

"You think, boss? Yeah, I didn't like him either. Rude brat!"

"The problem is that, if he is himself, he will tell everything to his grandfather and uncles. With that, my plan to buy those lands at a 'bargain price' could go down the drain! You know what, my faithful companions? The time has come to act and take drastic action."

"And what action is that, Colonel?" Tiao asked, all interested, showing a very sinister smile.

"Tomorrow, I want you two to get up early, get your weapons, and go to that old idiot's place. Do not let anyone see you; I want you to watch and wait for the first opportunity to kidnap someone in the family…"

"Kidnap someone in the family? But who? Could it be the old man?"

"No, Tiao…Not the old man! The idea is for you to catch the grandson imp, because, for sure, he is the darling of the family. However, if it is not possible, bring me one of the children…Remember: I want confidentiality. Do you understand?"

"Hmm, sort of! Why are we going to take the trouble of kidnapping someone from the farm if they don't have the money to pay the ransom? Wasn't it better for us to kidnap wealthy people?"

"Oh, what a stupid man! Isn't it possible, Tiao that you haven't understood until now? Pay attention that I will explain to both of you what my plan is!"

"Then explain it, Colonel, to see if I can understand now," said Tiao, all embarrassed.

"As soon as you bring whoever I asked for, I will immediately contact the old man to offer him an undeniable deal: the freedom of your dear relative in exchange for the sale of the farm. From what I know, you can't deny it!"

"But what if they call the police, claiming it was us?"

"Don't worry, Chico! The police and no sheriff will come to disturb me, they know very well who is in charge here in these regions…And they won't be able to prove anything either! That's why I want you to do everything without any testimony, do you hear?"

"Yes, sir! But, Colonel, what if they happen to be able to sell the plantations and come here to pay the ransom?"

"Ouch, Tiao! I must be very patient with you! Once and for all, understand *I am not interested in ransom money! What I want is the farm, those lands, as I said, are worth a fortune, understand?*"

"Oh! Yes. You can leave with us, Colonel. Tomorrow we will do everything well, as you say. If it depends on us, that farm is already yours!"

"Hmm. That's what worries me, Tiao!"

***

The stars were already shining in the sky, when the boys opened the gate of the farm, illuminating the path with the lantern. Grandma Maria, not restraining herself, ran to meet them and hugged them. Despite the hugs, she drew their attention so that they would no longer be absent the way they did, without the presence of an adult.

Grandpa Jorge, despite his frown, tried not to be too angry with the boys; he just told them that he didn't like this disappearance and that, next time, they would let him know where they were going.

Allan, seeing that his grandparents were right, apologized and added, "Grandpa, if we told you where we were going, surely you wouldn't let…We did it not for fun, but for a good cause!"

"Don't tell me that you tried to go on those hills?"

"No, Grandpa!" We went to Colonel Faustino's farm and discovered many, many things, mainly because of his interest in his lands!

"What! How crazy, you took too much risk! It is hard to even believe that they had that courage! Thank goodness that nothing happened; that man is the devil himself and would not think twice about harming them! Come in and take a shower. In a little while, we'll talk."

***

Later, as usual, everyone gathered in the front of the house. Grandpa Jorge pretended little curiosity, because he was still angry, and couldn't wait to hear what the boys had to report.

Uncle Milton, who was lying in a hammock, got up and went to pick an orange from a fruit bowl on the table. He also took a knife and started to peel it. When it was just before he finished, he stopped, looked at his nephew, and said,

"Allan, I also didn't approve of the attitude that you and Samuel had. They know very well that they risked too much to go to that bastard's farm. Not to mention the concern that you left us, disappearing for several hours…But I must agree that I admire the courage of you two, not only for this episode but for everything I have noticed! Well…thank God, nothing happened, but I confess to being very nervous and curious to know what information they brought from there!"

"Once again, Uncle, I want to apologize to everyone! It was not our intention to worry you. As I said before, we didn't go to play or to venture out; we went only to try to discover something that would show us the colonel's real interest in the farm. It is logical that we were aware of the risk; so, we were very careful to approach the window of the house, before we heard from the colonel himself that this place is worth a fortune…"

"What!" exclaimed Uncle Milton, widening his eyes, and dropping the orange and knife to the floor. "But how? I don't understand?"

Grandpa Jorge and Grandma Maria were paralyzed by the revelation of their grandson, while Uncle Alberto stood up immediately to pick up the knife and orange that his brother had just dropped.

"That's what you heard! The site is worth a lot of money…All because of a large deposit of uranium that is found there in the hills, just in the part that belongs to you, Grandpa."

"My God, I don't even know what that is! I had never heard of this uranium, much less that it existed in those parts…And how did they find out about it on my land?"

"Calm down, Grandpa, I'll explain everything! One of the main functions of uranium is in the construction of atomic bombs and in obtaining electrical energy. I have already heard my father talk a lot with his friends, and that is exactly what we heard from the colonel about the discovery of geologists."

"Geologists! Now I understand…those three who were here in the service of the federal government. That day, I warned them about the dangers in those mountains. I remember that only one of them came back alive. At the time, someone told me that he saw him running like crazy toward Colonel Faustino's farm and, a few days later, he was found dead floating in the river. Certainly, he was murdered, as his neck was cut and he had some injuries to his back. Several people commented that it was the scoundrel's work."

"And it was, Grandpa! I could hear very well the moment when he was remembering the appearance of the geologist. And as soon as he heard about the great discovery, he sent Chico the Ambusher to end the poor man's life."

"Rascal, murderer!" shouted Uncle Alberto, gesturing with the knife in his hand. "That pest had to rot in jail. The problem is that the sheriff here in the region always stands by him, covering up all his crimes, especially when there is no evidence. Our luck, as far as I know, is that a new sheriff is coming here. They said he is very efficient and does not let any crime go unresolved."

"Oh, thank God! We were really in need of an authority around here," said Grandma Maria, kissing a crucifix that hung around her neck.

"We must thank God, also for the good news that the boys brought us…I would never have imagined that our farm was worth a fortune! So, do you mean that our problems are solved? Let's sell that uranium right away and pay off all our debts!" argued Uncle Milton, his eyes shining with happiness.

"Calm down, Uncle. Don't be so excited! Uranium is not the same thing as a bag of coffee or corn that you sell on any street corner. Sometimes it can take a long time!"

"Did this pest even find a buyer for this deposit?"

"I don't think so, Mr. Milton," Samuel replied, all shy and afraid of being scolded. "I heard Colonel Faustino say that as soon as he has possession of that uranium, he will try to sell it to the Americans or to the Russians. It seems that the two currently are the most interested parties."

"Grandpa, I think the most certain thing right now is to put into practice everything that was agreed yesterday!"

"Once again, you are right, Allan! Alberto and Milton, tomorrow, as soon as possible, you will leave for Araxa, and if you happen to get nothing, you will immediately go to the state's capital. We need to sell everything we planted very quickly to resolve this situation once and for all! Now let's all sleep. Have a good night."

Chapter IX
The Kidnap

The next morning, as soon as the stars had disappeared from the sky, Uncle Milton and Uncle Alberto got up and went to get ready. They packed their bags, separated some documents, and then provided the cart. The neighing of one of the horses woke everyone in the house and, in a matter of minutes; they were already in the kitchen.

Grandma Maria, as always, made coffee, set the table, and went to check if the sons were forgetting something. She was very distressed and anxious, as she did not like to see them go far. Grandpa Jorge was also concerned. He took a candle and lit it near an image of the baby Jesus, asking for protection for his sons.

The boys helped to take the bags out of the house.

After everything was done, Samuel figured something out,

"Wait, are you going there by wagon?"

"Yes, until Araxa. But, if we need to go to Belo Horizonte, we will leave with some friends who, for sure, will take care of it for us," explained Uncle Alberto, holding the reins with one hand and with the other fixing his new hat on his head.

After Uncle Milton also got on the wagon, they said one last goodbye and left through the gate.

Allan, realizing the grandmother's sadness, picked up the most beautiful flower in the garden, which was right at the entrance to the farm, and handed it over with a hug and a tender kiss on the cheek. Then he called his friend to play and pick some fruits behind the house.

As soon as they climbed a guava tree, Samuel started to yawn in sleep and reported that he had not slept well last night, worried about the schedule. Allan, who until then was avoiding the subject so as not to upset his friend, ended up confessing the same fear, "I am also very worried, Samuel! My fear is that they might find it and come here to do some harm to my grandparents if they suspect us."

"Don't even tell me that, Allan! I don't even want to think that this could happen…If you want, we'll go there right now and look for it!"

"Hmm…I don't know, Samuel! I have some doubts about whether we should go. Yesterday we apologized to my grandparents, and I didn't want to disappoint them by disappearing again!"

"Yes, you are right! However, we must think that it is for a good cause!"

"Yes, I know! The problem is what excuse we are going to find to leave the place!"

"Wow, I didn't even think about it! And now?"

"I know, Samuel! Let's get a hoe and look for some worms."

"Worms? But for what? Tell me what you're up to?"

"As soon as we find some of them, we will tell my grandparents that we are going fishing and, as you know, all fishing takes a while…"

"You are a genius! So, let's get these little worms soon."

***

At that same moment, Uncle Milton and Uncle Alberto were anxiously following some trails that gave access to the highway. They wanted to buy time and avoid the movement of the local road, which was very dangerous.

Despite their nervousness, they talked about various subjects, sometimes even funny ones, making them forget a little about the real reason that led them to an uncertain destination. At other times, they were silent observing all the beautiful things that Mother Nature provided, thus giving a feeling of peace and tranquility.

But with only a few kilometers to go, something hidden behind some trees and bushes startled them and stopped them immediately.

"Well, well…How cute! Where do the bumpkins think they are going with these bags and luggage?" Chico the ambusher asked ironically pointing a revolver at the wagon.

"It's none of your business," replied Uncle Milton.

"Wow, but what a lack of manners," Chico quipped.

"I don't need to have any manners with people like you! And, after all, what are you doing hidden and armed behind these trees?"

"Answer him, Tiao!"

"We recognized the wagon from afar and then we hid and waited! For those who had to go to your farm to kidnap someone in the family, two are too good…It looks like it's our lucky day."

"You must be crazy, let us pass," said Uncle Alberto taking the whip to make the horses run away.

"You better drop that whip and be very quiet! My finger is dying to pull this trigger! Tiao, go up and tie them up…Let's use the wagon to take them to the boss."

At that moment, three people who had been walking through the woods noticed that movement and, understanding nothing, immediately hid in the bush to see what was happening. Only after the wagon sped away did they manage to say something,

"Oh, mighty god Tupa! It looks like that was a kidnapping. Protect my noble friends," said Mr. Acaua very concerned.

"Who are they, Dad?" Jaci, one of Mr. Acaua's daughters, asked.

"Those two who were caught are part of the family we were going to visit; and the other two who were armed, I also know them, they are dangerous bandits…"

"And now, Dad, what should we do?" The other daughter asked, very nervous.

"I will follow them, Irani! I want you two to be right here, quiet and carefree. I will not take long."

"But, Father, you cannot go alone. It's very dangerous! If you want to wait a while, Jaci and I will seek help there in the village."

"There won't be time. Rest assured! I will just watch where they are taking my friends."

More than quickly, Mr. Acaua went through the closed forest, as if he were a wild cat chasing prey. Despite his age, he was physically fit, as he was used to traveling long distances in the forest in search of game to support his family and the entire tribe. So, he had no trouble following, even if from a distance, the dust that the horses made on the road. Half an hour later, tired of running and dodging thorns and poisonous animals, he observed that the cart entered through a huge gate of a beautiful farm. He sneaked up without letting anyone see him and then looked for a good spot near the house to hide and try to understand what was going on. Anyway, after going under some bushes, he was immobile and could witness the colonel's every evil, whipping the prisoners mercilessly and praising his henchmen for their good work.

"Thank you, boss," replied Chico the Ambusher, all proud.

"I thought you were going to take the whole day to bring me a hostage, and then you brought me two."

"It was very easy, Colonel! When we were halfway there, we spotted the cart and waited. They were going to travel!"

"Yeah…You can tell, Tiao! Open the suitcases and I want to see what they were carrying."

"Right away, boss! Well, it looks like there are only clothes…No, it looks like there are some papers too!"

"Give me that, Tiao! Hmm. Let me see. Ahh! I was already expecting that."

"What is written there, boss?" Chico asked.

"Addresses of distributors and cooperatives in Araxa and the capital. These idiots wanted to outmaneuver me and sell the entire plantation over there…Bah! It seems like you don't know who you're dealing with. But now it's over. End of the line for both. If the old man doesn't give me the farm, I won't be sorry to kill you."

"Mongrel Dog! I hope that one day you and these bastards of your henchmen will burn in the fires of hell."

"Calm down, Alberto! There is no point in being nervous with this worm; it is a waste of time. From what I'm seeing, this time he won," said Uncle Milton. He was very bitter, looking seriously at his brother.

"Our father will never sell our land to you! Even more 'at a bargain price'," shouted Uncle Alberto very angry, not wanting to see that they had lost.

"Fool! It looks like you still don't understand. Not long ago, I would even pay for the farm. But now I want it in exchange for your life!"

"Cretin, you can't do this," shouted Uncle Alberto again.

"Enough! Keep quiet or I'll finish you right now! Tiao and Chico untie the two and lock them in the barn. If you try anything, shoot to kill!"

"I'll love doing that, boss," said Iron Fist Tiao, holding the gun.

At that same moment, the old Indian, not restraining himself with so much distress and anxiety, looked up to the sky and begged his god Tupa to enlighten him with great wisdom to help his friends escape, as quickly as possible, from those bandits. Coincidentally, a loud noise that came from the corral made him have a great idea; and, as soon as he saw that his friends had indeed been untied, he ran as fast as he could to frighten and make the cattle run away.

Realizing that the animals were running over everything they found ahead, the survival instinct spoke louder and made the colonel and his henchmen run to save their lives, finally giving the hostages a great chance to escape.

Disgusted with all that and seeing that the cattle were no longer dangerous, the colonel shouted, shouting with rage,

"Who was the idiot who left that gate open and where did my hostages go?"

"I don't know, Colonel," said Tiao, picking up the revolver on the floor.

"Look, Colonel! There go the bumpkins, see? They are getting into the woods," Chico informed him, pointing the gun.

"And what are you two waiting for, you idiots? Go after them and bring them, dead or alive!"

Afraid of being discovered and seeing that there was nothing more to do, the wise Indian decided to return and see his daughters. When he found them, he embraced them and said, "Come on…We have to go as soon as possible to let my friends' family know what's going on."

"Yes, Dad! But what about those men, how are they? They are well?" Jaci, who was still very nervous, asked.

"I can't say for sure, Jaci! I know that they managed to escape; I just hope that Tupa will help them to get out of those woods alive and that they will not be captured again by those evil men."

Almost everything on the farm was on track for Allan's plan to work. They caught several worms, separated some fishing rods, and had the permission of Grandpa Jorge. However, Grandma Maria was afraid and did not want to give an answer right away. Only after an hour did she decide to give her permission, if the boys promised that they would stay in a safe place by the river and that they would never, under any circumstances, enter the water to swim. After many, many promises, they put a reinforced snack in a bag, picked up all the material from the fishery, and ran in the direction of the gate. As soon as they closed it and took the first steps, they stopped and were paralyzed, momentarily, when they saw in the distance, three indigenous people waving and running toward them.

"My God! Who are those Indians?"

"Stay calm, Samuel! See, it looks like one of them is Mr. Acaua!"

"Wow, it's him! What a relief!"

"I'm glad he's coming to visit us, but I think our plan to go back to the colonel's farm went down the drain!"

"You're right, Allan! The way is to leave it for tomorrow! Are those two Indians who are coming with him his daughters?"

At that moment, Allan answered nothing. He was silent for a few seconds, seeming to sense something was wrong. Although he was still a boy, he knew it was not normal for someone to come in for a visit running desperately like that. But he tried to forget what he had thought, opened a big smile, and ran to embrace the old Indian, also accompanied by Samuel.

"It's good that you came to visit us! Who are these women?"

"These are my daughters, Allan. Jaci e Irani."

"Nice to meet you!" said the two boys at the same time.

"I'm happy to see you again, but I don't have good news!"

"My goodness," exclaimed Samuel.

"Come on. Let's go in and have a nice glass of water. My grandparents are inside and will enjoy the visit!"

Quickly everyone entered the farm. Allan, holding a fishing rod in one hand and appearing to be the most anxious, immediately shouted,

"Grandpa, Grandma…See who came to visit us! It is Mr. Acaua and his daughters."

"What a catch! Instead of bringing us fish, you brought us friends," joked Grandpa Jorge, smiling.

"Hello…Nice to meet you, Mr. Jorge and Mrs. Maria! I heard a lot about you. My name is Acaua and these are my daughters, Jaci and Irani. We are from a tribe here in the region."

"The pleasure is all ours! The boys and my sons talked too much about you and I was really looking forward to meeting you…In fact, all of us here on the farm already knew about the existence of your tribe, so much so that sometimes we see some Indians in these regions."

"Your daughters are very beautiful! And they are identical twins," Grandma Maria commented all kindly. "Come on…Let's go in and have some warm coffee."

"If you don't mind, we'd like a glass of water instead. We came running and we are very thirsty," said the old Indian, wiping sweat from his face.

"Certainly! Allan, bring the jar that the water is cool. Samuel, bring the glasses."

"Yes!" said the boys at the same time, eager to know the news that the Indian friend had come to bring.

"What a pity that my children are not! They would be happy with your visit…Boys, then you help me with the cups so I can serve the…"

"Mrs. Maria, the coffee will be for another day! Sorry for our rush, the news I bring is not very good! It's about your sons…Right now, they are trapped in a forest, and we must act very quickly, as they are at serious risk of death."

For a few seconds, everyone was extremely silent, perplexed by the news. Allan was the first to come out of that shock and, more than quickly, took a chair for his grandmother to sit on. Then he ran to the kitchen, got some sugar water to calm her down, because at that moment she was already in tears, shivering, and being supported also by Mr. Acaua's daughters. As soon as she calmed down, she herself asked the Indian to tell everything without hiding anything, after all, she always, throughout her life, knew how to face problems with a lot of guts and courage.

Before Mr. Acaua started, Grandpa Jorge, who, until that moment, had not been able to say a word, approached his wife, sat down beside her holding her hand, and only then, with a steady look, nodded that the Indian reported what he knew.

Samuel, unhappy with everything he had heard, was paralyzed for a few seconds in a corner of the room. He feared that what was happening was because of the lost pocketbook. With each report from his Indian friend, he grew paler and paler, with tears in his eyes and sobbing very quietly. It was only after Mr. Acaua finished telling everything, that he managed to say something, "My God! Poor things, they can't die. We must call the sheriff as soon as possible."

"Sheriff! But isn't he conniving with everything wrong that Colonel Faustino does in these parts? For sure, he will do nothing to harm him!"

"You're right, Allan! The worst is that the new sheriff will take a few more days to arrive…And now, my God, what are we going to do? One thing is certain: we cannot waste time. We must do something!"

"I already know, Mr. Jorge! Get us two horses and we'll go to my tribe as soon as possible. There I will gather several warriors and we will go heavily armed to the colonel's farm. I just want to see if he and his henchmen are real men seeing spears and arrows pointed at them."

"Thank you, Mr. Acaua! I think it was God who sent you here…I don't even know how to thank you. I hope that one day I can return the favor."

"You are welcome, Mr. Jorge! So, let's go now because we can't waste another minute. And you, my daughters, stay and wait for me to come back…Take care of Mrs. Maria and don't leave her alone."

"Yes, Dad," said the two sisters together, showing a sweet and sweet smile.

Grandpa Jorge quickly provided the animals and asked the boys to stay and help with whatever was necessary. Finally, after everything was taken care of, the two men hurriedly left for the village.

Sometime later, dozens and dozens of feather ornaments appeared behind bushes in the vicinity of the farm. Indians heavily armed and painted for war awaited only the order of their leader to invade and fight bravely without any fear of dying. Their war tactics were the same as those used for hunting. They communicated with each other imitating birdsong, and then they surrounded the enemy or the prey moving around, sneakily, like a jaguar among the foliage. Only when Mr. Acaua raised his spear, giving the signal, did they enter, all at once, and made the colonel and everyone who was there as prisoners.

"Where are my children, mangy dog? Speak soon, because I'm not kidding!" shouted Grandpa Jorge very angry, holding a very sharp knife.

"I don't know what you're talking about, old man! You must be crazy! And where did so many Indians come from? I thought that there were few who lived here in the region!"

"Don't make me lose my temper with you, devil! Do you think I'm not recognizing that wagon?! Come on, Mr. Acaua, tell him everything you saw!"

The old Indian, with all his experience, didn't even want to hear much talk. He knew that he was dealing with a bad person and that he would certainly deny everything. Then, more than quickly, he ordered his warriors to aim their spears and arrows to compel him to speak.

In his entire life, Colonel Faustino had never experienced such a situation. For years and years, it was always he who panicked and tortured everyone who opposed his will. Now he was there, intimidated, scared, and with none of his henchmen to defend him. Seeing that he had nothing more to do and that the situation was getting more and more out of control, he decided to say:

"Really, Mr. Jorge, your sons were here earlier today. But don't ask me to tell you why. I only know that they were startled by the cattle burst and then ran into the woods. I immediately asked my employees to go after them, as I was very concerned. But so far, none of your children and none of my employees have returned…I don't know what may have happened, but surely those forests hide many dangers and mysteries. I hope they all come back because I don't want any visitor to be harmed or complain about my hospitality…"

"Liar devil! I know perfectly well that you asked yourselves on the road and why this is so!"

"Do you really know, Mr. Jorge?"

"I'm not a fool, colonel! You are not interested in my property for nothing…Your real interest is in uranium, cretin!"

"Very well, Mr. Jorge! Your spies worked well! And since this is no longer a secret, I would like to offer you a partnership, a society…You come in with your lands and I with all my influence. I know important people not only in Brazil but in other countries that can help us to quickly commercialize this source of energy…We can become rich, just accept it!"

"It would be the last thing in the world that I would want. I would never accept to be a partner with a dishonest person like you. And, to tell you the truth, I'm not worried about wealth; I just want peace and have my kids back."

"What a pity, you bumpkin! If you don't want it for good, I will do it for bad!"

"That's what you think, scoundrel! Mr. Acaua, tell your warriors to tie this viper very well. We've already wasted too much time. Let's go search the entire farm and, if we do not find them, the way will be to look for all the forest."

A few hours passed and no trace was found. To make matters worse, the night was approaching, and, with the darkness, it became more difficult to find any clue. Despite the experience of the Indians, who stayed days and nights after hunting, they knew that they were dealing with dangerous bandits and decided to temporarily end their search to continue the next day as soon as possible.

The old Indian ordered the farm employees to be released because they had nothing to do with it. Then he ordered the colonel to be untied and arrested in the barn. Then he placed two lookouts on the door and others on different parts of the property. Finally, he approached Grandpa Jorge and said,

"I want to ask you to come back to the farm today to spend the night with your wife and reassure my daughters. Say, I'm fine and everything's under control. Tomorrow, you come back, and we are going to look for your children together again."

"Okay, I'll do it! At dawn, I'll be here. I won't be quiet until I find them! Good night and take care."

As soon as he arrived at the farm, Grandpa Jorge noticed that the lights outside the house had come on. Allan, who was at the window, saw his grandfather arrive and came with Mr. Acaua's daughters to help him out of the wagon.

"Thank you, guys. It was many, many years ago that I stopped being young like you! My arms are very sore; I think I'm losing my strength and my grip on the reins."

"Don't say that, Grandpa! It is still very strong and very healthy. But I see that you came back even sadder! What happened?"

"Excuse me intrusion, Mr. Jorge! But we are all here very concerned with everything that is happening. Tell us the truth. Where is my father and your sons?" Jaci asked, very anxious.

"Your father and all the warriors are fine! We take over the farm and everything is under control. My sadness is that I haven't found any trace of my sons yet. But I have a lot of faith that God will bring them back, safe and sound! My other concern is with Maria…Poor thing, she doesn't deserve to be going through this!"

"Your wife is nervous…She cried all day, but now she slept. We made her a very tasty soothing tea; it's a little secret from our tribe, made with herbs and roots. Its effect makes the person calm down and sleep for a long time," Irani explained, calmly, giving a beautiful smile.

"Where's Samuel?"

"He wanted to have some tea and ended up sleeping too, Grandpa."

"So, it really works! Listen, tomorrow I want to get up very early to return to the farm. I really want to be there to continue the search. And I would like to ask you to distract Maria a lot and give her more of this tea. I really want to wake her up tomorrow afternoon with our sons back! Now let's go in and have a good night!"

The next day, as soon as the sun came up on the horizon, everyone, except for Grandma Maria, had already risen.

Jaci made coffee and Irani prepared the table with some cookies, cake, cheese, and some fruits. Grandpa Jorge, in a hurry, had just a cup of coffee and went out quickly toward the wagon, being followed by the boys. As soon as he tried to climb, he felt a strong pain in his arms that made him fall out and fall sitting on the floor. Allan immediately helped him to his feet and asked him,

"Grandpa, are you okay? What happened?"

"Nothing my grandson. Do not worry! My arms are still very sore! I think I will have a hard time keeping track of the horses."

"Grandpa, I think you better not take any chances! Remember that time when you fell on the bank? Imagine if we weren't there to take it out; it could have been worse."

"You're right! I will never forget that…You two were amazing!"

"Mr. Jorge, how about we take you? We already got a handle on the reins and…"

"No, Samuel, thank you. I don't want to put them at risk."

"Grandpa, there's no risk! Samuel and I know how to control animals very well, and we are not going to stay…"

"We will take you to the colonel's farm and walk back. Do not worry; we already know the way quite a lot, not to mention that you yourself told us that everything is under control…Remember?"

"Yes! Thanks to God and to Mr. Acaua!"

"So, Grandpa, let us help…Unless you gave up on going!"

"Never! I can't wait to find my sons! Okay, you convinced me…Tell Jaci and Irani and let's go soon."

When they arrived at the farm, Grandpa Jorge wanted to know if there was anything new, as he was very hopeful that his sons might have shown some sign of life during the night. As soon as he heard that everything was still the same, he was saddened and went quietly under a tree to say a prayer without letting anyone see him cry.

The boys were very quiet from the moment they arrived, silently observing that scenario. Samuel barely breathed, every minute he became more worried and astonished, seeing, everywhere, heavily armed Indians, as if they were at war. Allan, on the other hand, focused his gaze only on the horizon. He knew there was something wrong because the forest was extremely calm. At no time did he see birds taking flight in fear or fright. This indicated that it was unlikely that his uncles were still around. Unless they have already been executed.

The old Indian quickly recruited the best warriors, gathered some things, and said,

"We are ready, Mr. Jorge! Let's go?"

"Yes. I can't wait to get into those woods again…I hope that God will light our way and help us find some clues about my sons! Ah, before I forget, I want you boys to go back to the farm immediately as arranged."

"Sim, Grandpa! We're on our way. Before, I just wanted to pick some fruit to eat on the way. I think our breakfast was very quick…"

"Okay. Goodbye and stay out of trouble! Mr. Acaua, let's go!"

The boys didn't even take a step until they were out of sight. They stood there, meditating and hoping that everything would work out. It was only after a few minutes that they went looking for the fruit and, despite having seen some very ripe, they continued to search, because their true intentions were different. They really wanted to stay there as long as they could, to discover something. They were calm; they knew that several warriors had stayed on the farm, taking care of everything. As soon as they passed by the barn, they were startled by a loud cry from the colonel, who was with his face in a small window.

"Brats! I know it was you who were here snooping around my property and went to tell the old man everything you heard about uranium. I suspected as soon as I saw that lost pocketbook…Wait until I get out of here! Everyone will pay dearly for it!"

"You are the one who will pay dearly for all your crimes…You bastard! And, if you are thinking that we are afraid of your threats, you are very wrong…"

"Allan, if you are not afraid, I am! And not to mention the sadness I've been feeling. I know very well that it is my entire fault! I knew that sooner or later, they would find that agenda," said Samuel very quietly.

"Stop being silly and let's go for another walk!"

"So, let's go, Allan, I don't want to be around this man anymore!"

They walked for half an hour inside the farm and then decided to stop under a tree to rest. The day was very hot and made sweat run all over the boys' faces.

Discouraged by the lack of clues and the unbearable heat, they thought of leaving, but a small sound of running water from behind the corral made them run there to cool off. The stream, which until then was new, made the search hopes reignite. The boys took off their shoes and walked slowly through the water, watching everything nearby. When they saw that they were about to enter the closed forest, they were afraid and decided, with great sadness, to end the search. As soon as they got out of the water and put on their shoes, one thing caught Allan's attention.

"Look, Samuel! There, right at the beginning of the forest…See?"

"Seeing what?"

"Those dented bushes and those little trees with some hanging branches!"

"Yes, I see! But what does it mean?"

"Samuel, someone or something passed by, and it seemed that he was in a hurry!"

"Ok! But it could be the cowboy with the cows!"

"Samuel, no cowboy is going to take cows to graze in a place like this!"

"Maybe some of them ran away and went into the woods!"

"It's possible! Let's get a little closer and look."

"Okay, Allan! But calm down, you don't have to walk so fast!"

"Look, Samuel, boot prints everywhere!"

"Yes, I see! And they seem to be of different sizes!"

"And did you notice that they are all heading toward the forest and that there is no trace of cows here?"

"Yeah!"

"And another thing…There is no Indian footprint!"

"Got it, Allan! Certainly, Mr. Acaua did not come by!"

"Samuel, what do you think about us going ahead and looking for more traces?"

"You are crazy! What if we get lost?"

"Do not worry! We will always follow the course of the stream and then just go back the same way…Got it?"

"Wow! You surprise me! I also think that I am too lazy to think! But then, what are we waiting for? Let's go!"

Despite not having machete or suitable clothes, they entered the bush without much difficulty. They were young and avoided any obstacle with great agility and courage. They were attentive to everything, and from time to time they stopped to admire the beauty and curiosities that a forest can provide monkeys, squirrels, toucans, and even ocelots. Sometimes, the forest darkened with the lack of sunlight, and, in those moments, they were frightened by some small snakes, frogs, and several species of spiders. But nothing made them give up. It did not take long; they heard a strong sound of the current and saw a small stream that followed flowing into the great river. Finally, they approached the shore cautiously and soon saw something that tormented them…

"My God! Boot and slip marks…Samuel, some people probably fell into the river!"

"They fell or they threw themselves! It could be that they were running away from something or someone…And look at those other brands of boots; they head toward those tied boats! Let's have a look."

Allan, at that moment, suspected what had really happened, and went to approach the boats to confirm what he already imagined.

"Look, Samuel, more marks on the ground! There was certainly one more boat here and they pushed it into the river."

"Yes, I see! But what do you think happened?"

"I think my uncles had no choice and jumped into the water to save themselves. Certainly, the colonel's henchmen took a boat to catch up with them."

"Hmm, I think you're right, Allan. And now, what are we going to do?"

"We will hardly find my grandfather and Mr. Acaua in these woods to be able to warn them. The problem is that my uncles may be downstream at this hour, in urgent need of help…And that if the worst has not happened!"

"God help them!"

"Samuel, I know that at these times it is important to have faith, but we also must have an attitude…I will take one of these boats and go down the river. If you don't want to go, no problem!"

"Leave you alone? Never! If we get here together, we will go together until the end. My only concern with these oars; I don't have much practice."

"Stay calm, Samuel. I learned to paddle with my father in the countless fisheries that we did together and, besides, the river is very calm!"

"Well, I trust you and I hope God helps us too!"

They quickly untied one of the boats and pushed it into the water. As soon as they saw that there was nothing wrong, they went in and started down the river. Despite Allan's calm and excellent maneuvers, Samuel was in a panic, fearing that at any moment they might sink or hit a submerged log. Only after seeing that his friend really knew what he was doing, did he calm down and ask his friend to teach him how to row.

Chapter X
Unraveling the Mysteries

An hour passed and they found no trace of the whereabouts of Uncle Alberto and Uncle Milton. Head down and very upset, the boys rejoiced when in a curve they saw, in the distance, the farm and the daughters of Mr. Acaua. For a few seconds, they slowed the boat and kept their eyes fixed on the entrance to the house, hoping to see who they were looking for. Realizing that everything was the same, and not wanting to return without any information, they decided to continue with the searches, hoping to find some sign.

Twenty minutes after investigating the margins inch by inch and finding nothing, they decided to stop and go home. However, when they saw a very sharp curve with many rocks and tree branches scattered in the water, they decided to go there to make one last attempt. As soon as they entered this new path of the river, Allan was greatly surprised and frightened to see that his uncle Alberto's hat was right on the banks and at the feet of that mysterious hill.

"My God! Do you see that, Samuel!"

"My goodness…It's the hat you bought!"

"Yes, but that's not all. Look," said Allan standing on the boat, raising one arm.

"I see nothing but the hat. Come on; tell me, you're already making me worried! What else do you see?"

"Samuel, I can't believe you haven't realized where my uncles ended up so far!"

"My God! I can't believe we ended up here next to this haunted place…Allan, please, let's go now. We will ask for help. These hills are cursed and as far as I know, no one gets out of there alive!"

"Samuel, I know that you are very scared, and I will not lie saying that I am not. However, if we want to ask for help from my grandfather and Mr. Acaua, it will take us a couple of hours to return to the colonel's farm and, even so, maybe, we won't even find them…One thing is certain, in this life, we have to face our fears, even more if it is for a good cause."

"Allan, are you trying to say that you really decided to venture into these mountains?"

"Yes, I am! For my uncles, I do anything."

"Allan, I will confess to you that I am in a panic, but I am aware that part of all that is happening is my fault. If you go, I will go too and I hope that everything we have heard of this place is a mere rumor."

As soon as they disembarked, the boys tried to tie the boat to a tree with a very strong trunk. They did not want, under any circumstances, to miss that vessel, which was, without a doubt, the only way to return home. Then Allan took his uncle's hat and checked it for blood. Seeing that there was nothing, he calmed down a little and put the object in a corner of the boat.

Samuel was terrified, his hands were shaking, and he was sweating cold. At all times, he looked everywhere for fear of seeing something that frightened him. He wanted to run from there, get on the boat, and go home immediately, but his conscience wouldn't let him. Then he took a deep breath, created courage, and asked his friend,

"So, Allan, what's the plan? Have you thought of anything?"

"Not yet, Samuel! Immediately, I noticed that the mountains here are very steep and I saw only one path so far, there on our left side. See?"

"Yes, I am! And the good thing is that the woods there are not so closed."

"Samuel, the only thing that worries me is that up there can be an immensity of forests and trails that give access to various places. I think we should be marking the path very well so that we don't run the risk of getting lost. The idea is to go breaking and putting some tree branches and stones all along our path to signal. Only then will it be easy to return and reach the boat safely."

After everything was analyzed, they followed that part that was apparently the easiest. At first, the boys tried to walk very slowly, watching carefully from all sides. Sometimes they stopped and looked back suspiciously, afraid that something might be following them. Seeing that, until then, there was nothing that could scare them; they decided to walk faster and with more confidence, putting into practice everything they had agreed. Despite being young, they acted seriously, showing competence and a lot of calm to solve that problem that, until then, was very complicated. His determination was such that neither the hot sun nor the few shadows along the way made them slow down on that endless climb. Finally, after so much sweat, they arrived on a kind of plain that looked more like an oasis. Its extensive and dense vegetation, composed of immense trees, some fruit, others floriferous, differentiated it and much from other large plateaus that are normally areas with low vegetation. Undoubtedly, it was a very mysterious place; it seemed that someone had planted it all with the intention of hiding and camouflaging some things.

Despite that mystery, the boys did not want to give up…They went on, entered that forest, and sat under a tree to rest. Suddenly, something unexpected and very strange happened. Beams of light, reminiscent of the phenomenon of the northern lights, began to appear in all the shadowy parts of the forest, mainly in the crown of the big trees. Surprised, the boys got up as quickly as possible and watched it without understanding anything. Then, when they heard loud and terrifying roars, they were really scared, fearing that some big animal or something supernatural was there and put them in a possible risk situation.

The moment they were about to run, everything went back to normal as if by magic. For a few seconds, they were very quiet and immobile, thinking that all that would be repeated, but they heard nothing more and the only light they could see was that of the sun.

"That is a strange thing, Samuel! It looked like something ghostly…Did those roars have anything to do with the lights?"

"It might be! But the only thing I'm sure of now is that we should get out of this place as soon as possible!"

"Samuel, I know that you are nervous, and I do not think you are wrong…But I would love to find my uncles because they are important to me and my whole family."

"I understand! But I think we're going to need help. This saw is very dangerous and there are some things here that we don't understand…"

"I know! And that is also one of the reasons why I would like to stay! I really wanted to know what really happens here."

"There is certainly an explanation, Allan! But I think that, if we get too involved in this subject, we could get burned."

"Yes, I agree! But, at one time or another in life, we must take a risk, don't you think?"

Samuel didn't even have time to answer; he froze momentarily, looking like he was in shock. His pale expression, with wide eyes and a half-open mouth, showed that he wanted to speak and shout to his friend what he was seeing.

Allan looked back quickly and saw the reason for his friend's shock. Figures with human forms came toward them as if they were ready for battle. They held spears, knives, and some amulets. Most impressive of all they were wrapped with white linen bands that covered almost the entire body. Their faces, except for one that wore a mask shaped like a dog's head or a jackal, were borne, clearly showing the dry, dark, and slightly deformed skin.

Allan, as soon as he looked back at his friend, saw him already leaving and, to complicate matters, in the opposite direction to the boat, getting deeper and deeper into that forest. Not wanting to lose sight of him, he ran as fast as he could, shouting at him, "Wait, don't go there!"

Only after he stumbled on a rock and rolled violently over some bushes did Samuel realize that he was lost and getting more and more complicated, running that way aimlessly. When he saw his great friend approaching, with no one chasing him, he was a little more relieved and said, "Thank goodness you came after me!"

"Samuel, are you okay? Are you hurt?"

"No, Allan. I just skinned my knee a little…But I'm scared to death! What were those things?"

"I don't know for sure. But they looked like Egyptian mummies!" Allan said.

"Egyptian mummies! But what are you talking about!"

"Yes. In ancient Egypt, after death, several important people had their bodies prepared with some substances and linen bands to preserve. The one with the mask of the god Anubis represented death! I know because I already read that in my father's book."

"My God! Dead people walking…Now I really want to leave and…"

As soon as he finished speaking, Samuel grasped his friend tightly when he saw those mysterious creatures appear again from nowhere, surrounding them in a perfect circle. As they approached, a detail caught Allan's attention…The boy immediately took a tree branch from the ground and ran toward the leader with the intention of facing him. Mysteriously as they appeared, they disappeared without leaving any indication that they were there.

"Well, just as I suspected!"

"What did you suspect? And where did they go?" Samuel asked, shaking and almost crying.

"They didn't go anywhere! They don't even exist! Someone here is trying to scare us with these false images as if it were a movie."

"But how did you suspect that?"

"One of them, when approaching us, crossed a tree as if it were not there…Ghosts do not exist, and only an image with special effects could do that!"

Suddenly, something without explanation appeared and left that theory totally bankrupt, making everything a great mystery again. They were two huge animals that seemed to dispute the same game, and because they were so big, they broke small trees without any difficulty.

"Samuel, now it's time to run! Let's get back to the boat very quickly, as it looks very real."

"My God, please help us." Samuel was in tears.

"Come on, follow me, I remember the way."

The signs left to mark the way have greatly facilitated the boys' return to the boat. Despite being tired, sweaty, and with some abrasions on their bodies, they managed to find the strength to untie and push the vessel into the water. Allan, before entering, stopped, looked back, and said,

"I will return here with or without help…For my uncles I do anything!"

"Come in, buddy that those animals can get here anytime," said Samuel, very startled, still hearing the loud roar of one of them.

"Let's go!"

Only after he gave the first strokes, did Allan begin to reflect on all those events that had no meaning. Bitter because he did not understand anything and because he was unable to resolve what he wanted most, he said to his friend, "Samuel, I am very upset that we are going home without any indication that they may be alive. But, at this moment, what most intrigues me are the things that we witnessed. None of that had any logic…Everything was very enigmatic!"

"Enigmatic? As well?"

"These are difficult things to understand! For example, mummies that walk and then disappear…This is not normal! And those huge animals? I don't know if I'm mistaken, but the one who was ahead looked like a giant prehistoric bear and, as I recall one of our history classes, he was extinct more than twelve thousand years ago! The other one that was right behind, I don't know if you noticed, it was a dinosaur…Say if that has an explanation!"

"Well, Allan, I made no effort to know what kind of animals they were. I only know that they were huge and with deafening roars. But there was something that caught my attention: they seemed to be following something, and it certainly wasn't us."

"Weird, were they…"

Even before Allan could finish his speech, a childlike scream in a tone of despair echoed in those surroundings, followed by an intense noise, as if someone or something had fallen or been thrown into the water.

"Did you hear that, Allan?"

"Yes. Look, Samuel, there's a boy drowning back there, right next to where we were!"

"My God, now what?"

"Take the oars, Samuel. If I go swimming, I will arrive faster to save him."

"Okay but be careful!" Samuel spoke, concerned to see his friend preparing to jump into the river.

Allan has always been exceptional in swimming. At school Olympics, he always got along well in this modality, because he had experience and technique to swim in deep places like Olympic pools and rivers. Then, as soon as he dived, he immediately put into practice everything he knew to approach and pull as quickly as possible the boy who, at that moment, only had one arm out of the water, surrounded by algae and foliage from all over the type. Finally, when he managed to take him to the bank and rid him of so many branches and leaves, Allan could see clearly what he had just saved…

"My God, what are you?"

For a few seconds, a great silence reigned in that place. Seeing that he would get no answer, Allan immediately waved to his friend to come with the boat as soon as possible and see what he was witnessing.

"Allan, thank God you managed to save him! It took me a while because I still didn't get the hang of it with the oars. But after all who is this boo…My goodness, what is that!"

"Honestly, I don't know what it is. I don't think he talks, or he doesn't want to talk. I feel very sorry for him, because he is all hurt, cold and very afraid."

"Allan, he is very weird! The head is very large, out of proportion to the body, and the skull is elongated. Look at the mouth and nose, they are very small, but the eyes are huge and red, not to mention the skin that is very gray," Samuel described it, looking him up and down while tying the boat to a tree.

"One thing is certain, he is not a human, and he is not a hominid, much less an animal! I think he is a…"

Suddenly a voice, somewhat robotic, coming from the top of a bluff, interrupted Allan, "Thank you for saving our son. We will be grateful to you for all our eternity!"

"My goodness, they are the parents, and they are very similar! But, regardless of anything, let's get on the boat and get out of here as soon as possible!"

"Stop being afraid, Samuel! It looks like they won't do us any harm. After all, we saved their son!"

"You saved! What if they decide to *catch me*?"

"Be quiet, my friend, they have already come down and are coming here…Remember: you are with me!"

As soon as they approached, the tallest one, appearing to be the father, immediately put one finger on his own forehead, closed his eyes, and started to concentrate. Suddenly, a light shone brightly around his body and, looking like a kind of magic, made his son, who until then was lying in a place of difficult access, come floating close to him and stay there, immobile and levitating.

Then the other, of shorter stature, appearing to be the mother, quickly removed a bottle from her belt and poured a greenish liquid on the boy's wounds. In a matter of seconds, looking like a miracle, all wounds healed without leaving scars or any other marks.

Seeing that the son had really improved, the one who appeared to be the father ended the levitation process and put him on his feet. Then he stared at Allan and, again, said to him, "We would like to thank you again for saving you…What is your name?"

Allan was silent for a few seconds; he was astonished by everything he had just witnessed and, at the same time, intrigued by those unknown beings.

Realizing then that they would not hurt them and were there in peace, showing thanks, he reassured himself and replied,

"My name is Allan…Allan Smith. And this is my friend Samuel."

"And what are you doing here?" He continued to ask.

"We came looking for my uncles, Alberto and Milton…They were being chased by two dangerous bandits who wanted to kill them. On the run, they fell into the river and ended up here!"

"We saw the hat of one of them, right there on the bank," Samuel added, still afraid and very worried.

"I am in awe of you both, as well as speaking the truth; you have shown attitude and intelligence since the moment you arrived here. One thing that caught our attention was your courage, Allan. You faced the mummies bravely and then risked your own life, jumping in the river to save my son…This heroic act makes us always have admiration and an eternal debt to you!"

"But how do you know all this? And who are you?" Allan asked, very curious.

"I will answer you already. I just ask the two of you to keep secret from everything that I will tell you."

"You can trust us," replied, immediately, Allan.

"We give our word," completed Samuel.

"Well, my name is Zoorak BYM. This is my wife Zurlly WRN, this is my son Zuur WKL. We are from a small distant planet that is several light years from here, located in the constellation of Orion. My people have maintained a base on this mountain for thousands of years…We chose this planet because it serves as a bridge to other constellations and because it offers us water, food, oxygen, a good temperature, and uranium, which is the main base of the fuel. In addition to my family, others are also here. Each has its function, dedicating itself entirely to research on animal and plant life and on the usefulness of each ore existing here on this planet. My wife and I were chosen to manage all the work and, above all, to keep any intruders away!"

"My God, what a fantastic story! You mean you are really aliens?" Samuel asked, seeming not yet to believe.

"Call us however you want! I think we're just your neighbors."

"Wow! Even if I wanted to tell, no one would believe," Samuel continued. "But why did your son fall into the river? What went wrong?"

"It was an accident! Or rather, a big mistake of mine! Well, before explaining what happened, I would like to make it very clear that our intention here is not to make anyone die, but rather to be afraid…Death is a consequence of despair, sometimes it is because they do not know how to swim or hit their head on a rock or something…The truth is that, from the moment you arrived, my purpose, as always, was to make you run away or enter the…Well, never mind! As I was not able to, I decided to release one of the animals to see if it had any success…"

"When releasing the young tyrannosaurus, I also activated the door of the big bear, but my son was there, feeding the animal. With the shock, he did not even remember that he could dominate the animal with high technology and, instead, ran in despair making the two animals see him as prey…to save himself, he threw himself into the river, completely forgetting that I didn't even know how to swim. The truth is that no one of my people knows, and if it weren't for you being around, for sure, I would be without my son now. One thing is for sure, we must always pay close attention to everything we do so that we don't have a headache."

"Accidents do happen, Zoorak! The luck is that my friend Allan knows how to swim very well," Samuel spoke.

"Yes, accidents happen, but this is a rare case here. Apart from today's event, only one fact, which occurred many, many years ago, has been recorded! Another team that was here made, practically, the same mistake…Instead of releasing two animals to chase away miners who were here, they released three. The whole problem was that one of them was flying and was hungry. It was a huge Pterosaur that could never, under any circumstances, have been released. The men, who had never seen anything like it before, jumped into the river in a panic and drowned. The animal, seeing that it had not managed to catch any of them, flew from here and ended up in an indigenous tribe attracted by the large number of fish caught by the Indians. To rescue him, it took a large ship to pull him and bring him back…"

"Wow, did you hear that, Allan? It is the same story that your uncles and Mr. Acaua told. So, it was true!"

Allan, who until then had been silent just listening, decided to question some things that were still mysteries,

"Zoorak, I just don't understand one thing…Why do some things here seem to be real and others unreal? Ghosts, walking mummies…That doesn't exist! The animals, yes, looked quite real, but what intrigues me most is that they have been extinct for thousands of years! What is there that we still don't know?"

"Very well! You are an intelligent and observant boy…I thought this was going to go unnoticed, but I was wrong. In fact, we use several methods to scare and chase away curious and adventurous people…Hauntings, skulls and mummies are merely illusions. We just put some special effects to give life, and, with that, people are quite frightened, simply, because they are afraid of supernatural things…Animals are real, and only in specific cases do we let them go. This usually happens when an intruder resist leaving, but in the end, the result is always the same…To avoid being devoured, jump in the river or run toward the time portal…"

"Did you say time portal?"

"Yes, Allan. My people have been using this resource for many, many years for time travel. Our goal is to pass on knowledge and research in general to ancient peoples. It is also for him that we bring these animals, now extinct, for all our interests."

"Time travel! That's cool!" said Samuel, all euphoric.

Allan did not show much euphoria. I was sad and very worried. Her heart was tight, and a tear was stubbornly rolling down her face. Thrilled and afraid, he asked, "And my uncles, what happened to them? Were they killed by these beasts or…"

"Your uncles and those who pursued them entered the portal of time."

"But now…What will happen to them? Where did they end up?"

"I'm sorry, Allan! What will happen to them or if they are still alive, I have no way of knowing. The only thing I can find out is where they ended up! Come with me."

After about ten minutes of walking through a closed forest, they came to a clearing with very few trees. Zoorak soon made a sign pointing where he was in the habit of opening the portal and, as soon as they approached, he said,

"Stay close to me, boys. I'm going to trigger it…Just need to touch a device here on my bracelet."

Suddenly, out of nowhere, a magnificent portal appeared in front of everyone. The boys gaped for a few moments, admiring that high technology that looked more like a mirage or a powerful magic. The lights around it was so bright and so diverse that they made a huge show of it all. In the center, it seemed to have a single whitish color that was a compact cloud that insisted on hovering inside.

"That's cool! It's incredible! But how do you manage to bring and pass giant animals there?"

"Good question, Samuel! The portal has several devices that allow us to make it the size we want and the time we want to go to. There, the animal, small or large, is attracted to enter it."

"Zoorak, but if you program it, what happens when someone enters without setting a specific date?"

"Another good question, Allan! The portal itself chooses a date at random…But don't worry, it contains a history of information that allows us to know where they went and even the photo of the people or animals that entered it…Come on, I'll show you."

Again, Zoorak pressed something on his bracelet and in a corner of the portal, a small screen with letters and numbers on its footer appeared. Immediately he typed in a few things and soon the image of four men appeared, who, of course, the last to enter there were.

"Look at these two here, they are my uncles!"

"And look at the other two. Iron Fist Tiao and Chico the Ambusher… Bandits," said Samuel.

"Allan, I have good and bad information to give you!"

"Okay…Say it, Zoorak. I'm ready!"

"I already found out where your uncles went…However, each went to a different age and, worst of all, accompanied by these bandits."

"Please, Zoorak, tell us soon. Where did they go?" Allan asked concerned.

"Well. According to your calendar, this one went to Rome in 80 AD. And this one, with the lightest hair, ended up in 1465 AD in Cusco, the capital and sacred city of the Inca civilization in Peru."

Allan, upon hearing Zoorak's reply, was stunned and apprehensive. He wanted not to believe it, but he knew perfectly well that it was real and, at the very least, tragic. Stopping at a time when customs, languages, beliefs, and thoughts were completely different could be a huge problem, especially with someone who did not deserve any kind of praise.

"Is there any possibility of bringing them back?" Samuel asked sadly, seeing his best friend's bitterness.

"Hmm. Yes! But it is not a very easy task."

Suddenly, Allan's eyes shone, and a smile of joy stood out on his face. Knowing that there was still a small hope of seeing his uncles again was all he wanted to hear.

"But what must be done, Zoorak? If you need, you can count on me!"

"Calm down, Allan! As I said, it is not simple, but very dangerous!"

"For my uncles, I will do anything!"

"It's ok! Follow me…I will take you to my people's control base to pick up something essential for this mission."

Again, everyone entered the forest and followed a narrow path. A few minutes later, they stopped in front of a rocky elevation with rocks so high and steep that it was almost impossible to climb. Zoorak immediately put his finger to his forehead, concentrated, and spoke a few words, very quietly.

Looking like a fairy tale, one of these huge stones crept up, giving rise to a secret entrance, all lit up and with a huge corridor that was out of sight. Its walls, in addition to being covered with beautiful granite, had large, refrigerated air equipment and several monitoring screens that transmitted, in real-time, everything that happened there. The floor was finished with large marble blocks interspersed with different stones looking like emeralds, ruby, sapphire, and amethyst. But the most interesting of all is that there were vehicles resembling mini-aircraft that floated on long, narrow tracks.

"Come on, boys; let's get in one of the vehicles, as they are the fastest way to get to the center of the base."

"Cool! I had never seen one of these in my life."

Samuel was all euphoric. "And how do they manage to stay afloat?"

"It's very simple! So much so that my people have already used this resource for many, many years…This is nothing less than magnetism or magnetic levitation, as you want to call it!"

"Magnetic levitation!"

"Yes, Samuel! They are powerful magnets that make vehicles fly over the tracks, and because there is no friction, they travel smoothly at incredible speeds."

"Gosh, I didn't understand anything! But let's go on that one, it is much more beautiful!"

"You're the boss," said the alien, admired by the boy's candor.

As soon as they arrived, the boys soon got off that 'car of the future', marveling at everything they saw. There were so many things to see that they didn't even know which way to look, let alone where to go. Zoorak introduced them to his people and asked his wife and son to keep company for the visitors while he went to get the object that was the reason they were there.

"See, Allan, how many lights and electronic devices and…look at this machine here, some reports are coming out of it. What is written? We will see…"

"You can't understand, Samuel. Their alphabet is completely different from ours…It looks like a mixture of ancient Egypt with Chinese…And look there too, huge screens for monitoring various points of the hills."

"Look, Allan, over there in that room! How many microscopes and test tubes…Certainly, there must be several research here."

"Certainly! And look at that other room over there…It has several huge capsules that look like freezing. I think those animals are being preserved to be studied! If they are not dead, they must be in a state of hibernation."

Zurlly, Zoorak's wife, seeing the boys' interest in everything, invited them to go to other rooms further on to show them another research.

"I want to show you our genetics research lab. Here we study the genetic code of several living beings, such as heredity and inherited diseases. Furthermore, we do a very good job of cloning and…"

"Did you say cloning?"

"Yes, Allan. Identical and perfect copies of any living species…Not to mention organ creation and the regeneration of mutilated limbs."

"Wow, that's so cool! Does that mean that if any of us here lost a body part, we could have it back?"

"Yes, Samuel."

"Unbelievable!!"

"But the best is what I am going to show you now! Look, can you see it in the corner of the room?"

"I do not see anything! Or rather, just a little mouse on the table, it seems to be dead."

"And is dead, Samuel! See, I'm going to give this injection to the mouse and wait a minute…"

"Hmm…nothing is happening!"

"Wait, Samuel! I said a minute, look!"

"My God. I must be dreaming! The rat lived again…But how?"

"We spent years studying this formula and, finally, just under a month ago, we achieved the long-awaited result."

"Everything here is amazing! It's hard to even believe," said Allan admiringly, watching the little animal run from side to side.

"Come on, let's go over to the front room, I'm going to show you something very interesting. Go ahead, the door is not locked!"

"What are these cabins for, Zurlly? And what does this little monkey do in there?"

"They are teleportation machines, Allan. They are very similar to the time portal; what sets them apart is that they do not send anyone to the past or to the future…See, just press this button here and the little animal ended up on that other machine in the front…"

"Awesome!! I once read a science fiction magazine that reported this…Now I see that it is possible!"

"Yes, it is possible, Allan."

"I'm fascinated by everything I've seen so far, Zurlly. I think that when you travel in the past, some people must think that you are a kind of God!"

"Yes, Allan. It happens a lot!"

"What's that in the corner of the room? It looks like an incubator and with stones inside?"

"Yes, Samuel. And you see that liquid that drips on them? Well, that is a new formula that we are researching. I believe that in a year we can have some results…Our goal is to be able to transform a common rock into gold. We use this metal a lot in almost all of our electronic devices…"

Zurlly had barely finished speaking and little Zuur pushed a button on the panel causing a secret door to open and give access to a huge hangar.

"Oh my! Look at that, Allan! I never thought that one day I would see a flying saucer, even more so close!"

"Me neither, Samuel! And it is huge…Fabulous!"

"Take us for a ride, Zurlly. I've never been on one of those!"

"In another opportunity, Samuel…And, in a little while, it will be replenished with a new load of uranium…Do you see those stairs up there?"

"Yes, we are!" replied the boys at the same time.

"Downstairs, on the lower floor, is where our uranium plants are located; there all the enrichment work is done to obtain energy."

"Cool! And where does that flying saucer leave from here…I don't see any way out!"

Just as Zurlly was about to explain, Zoorak appeared and said, "Come on, boys…I found what I was looking for! Now the success of this mission depends only on you!"

"What did you bring, Zoorak?"

"This is a bracelet, Allan. But is not any ordinary bracelet! It has devices like mine but with much more advanced technology."

"And what did you bring that for?"

"It's for you to use…You will need it a lot to be able to bring your uncles back."

"I'm glad you trust me, Zoorak!"

"As I told you before, Allan, I will always have eternal gratitude and trust for you."

"Thanks! But…What about my friend Samuel? Won't he need it?"

"Unfortunately, we only had one reserve, but I assure you that one is enough!"

"But how does it work?"

"I'll explain it to you, Allan! But first put them on your arm and press the white button."

"There, I already put it! But what is this little white button for?"

"As soon as you press, it will, in a matter of minutes, read all of your genetic code, such as your blood type, the color of your skin, all the details in your eyes, and even the tone of your voice…In short, it will have all entire DNA."

"But why is that Zoorak?"

"It's a matter of security, Allan! From now on, until the last day of your life, it will obey only you…"

"But how come…Will it be mine forever?"

"Yes! In addition to being a gift from you to me, this bracelet, as I explained to you, will only obey you. If one day you don't want it anymore, it will automatically lose all its functions!"

"Interesting! I mean each one of you here has his own bracelet?"

"Yes! Since the first years of our life, we use this technology daily…"

"It's ok! I just hit the white button…What now?"

"Well, let's go back to the place where we have the habit of activating the time portal. By the time we arrive, the bracelet will have already recorded all your data. There I will explain in more detail how it works, okay!"

"Yes. Then let's go!" said Allan, staring at that novelty in his arm.

The way back seemed to be endless for the boys. They were very anxious to arrive and open that magnificent portal that gave access to fantastic eras. To be able to go back in time was all they wanted, especially to places that had so many historical events and great achievements for humanity. As soon as they approached, Allan immediately recognized the area and immediately ran to the right spot saying,

"Here is the location! Isn't that right, Zoorak?"

"That's right, Allan. You have a great memory!"

"And now what do I do?"

"Calm down, I'll explain everything! Press the white button again, if it glows, it is already working…"

"Yes, it shone!"

"Okay. So, from now on he is ready to fulfill almost all your wishes!"

"But how so?"

"It's very simple, Allan! The technology of these bracelets is so advanced that they are able, through waves of energy, to multiply the power of your mind thousands and thousands of times. Just focus and you will achieve incredible things with just the power of your thoughts."

"Are you serious?"

"Yes, Allan…And, as I said on another occasion, that bracelet is more advanced than mine. You don't need to bring it close to your forehead like I sometimes do; just focus and go! Now, if you point to what you want or raise your hand, for sure, the strength of your mind will become even stronger."

"Wow! Come on, Allan, think of something. Can you levitate?" Samuel spoke excitedly and curiously.

"Not only will he be able to levitate, but he will also be able to fly you both!"

"You can only be kidding, Zoorak," said Samuel with wide eyes.

"I would never play with something like that! I know it seems impossible for you, but it is not!"

Allan knew that the alien was telling the truth. Then, more than quickly, he took Samuel's hand, closed his eyes for a few moments, and thought positively that they were going to fly. Suddenly, in a matter of seconds, they began to float to the top of a huge tree.

"That's so cool!" the two boys said at the same time. They had fun as if they were in an amusement park.

"You can let go of his hand, Allan! You just must want him to keep flying," Zoorak spoke, admired by the boys' joy.

"Wow, I really wish my parents and the school class were here, now, watching us, because if I tell them one day, they will think I'm crazy!"

"Look, Samuel, a thrush couple came flying close to us, and look down there, how small everything is."

"Yes, it is! And from up here, you can see almost all the hills."

"You know, Samuel...I, like you, would very much like my family to be around, and I also wanted a person that I already miss very, very much."

"Oh...I know! It's Jessica..."

"Yes. It's her!"

"Look, Allan. It looks like Zoorak is waving at us..."

"Yes. So, let's go down!"

"Ah...What a shame!"

As soon as the boys came down, Zoorak came over and said to them, "So, did you like the experience?"

"SOOO much! Can we go again? It's so cool!"

"Calm down, Samuel! Let's hear what Zoorak has to say."

"Boys, I didn't want to disturb your fun, but I advise you to be quick!"

"Why are you telling us this? Do you know anything?"

"Stay calm, Allan. I'm just afraid that, because your uncles are in periods of time where visitors were seen as enemies, anything can happen!"

"For sure, Zoorak! If it's up to me, I'm ready..."

"I'm too!" said Samuel looking up, remembering the unforgettable flight.

"Zoorak, did you miss telling me what this yellow button is for?"

"I was about to tell you! Well, as my people travel a lot in time, we adapted this little yellow button on the bracelets to open and close the portal."

"And how do I do it?"

"Press once to open and twice to close."

"Sounds easy! But what about that screen that you clicked to get some information about my uncles...This is where I must type the year and the place where I want to go, right!"

"Yes! Your bracelet has already been adapted so that, when you open the portal, this screen appears automatically...And don't worry, it is very easy to handle. Not to mention that you will have the option to type anything using your own alphabet."

"You made me think of something very important, Zoorak. How am I going to talk and find out about my uncles if there, in these places, the languages were completely different?"

"Very simple, Allan! It's the same way that I communicate with you!"

"What do you mean?" Samuel asked, puzzled by that.

"My language doesn't sound like yours either...I can only understand you and speak the same language, thanks to the bracelet...It's like telepathy."

"But did I hear you talking to your people in our language?"

"That's because you were close, Samuel...When we are alone, we use only our vocabulary."

"So already know, Allan...In these places, you will be my interpreter!"

"Don't worry, Samuel! Well, I think we're ready, Zoorak!"

"One more thing boys. When you enter the portal, the time clock works differently. Twelve hours in each era correspond to only one hour here!"

"Cool! Does it mean that if we stay there twenty-four hours, it will only be two hours here!"

"Exactly, Samuel! Oh, and not to mention that I didn't give you anything, take this with you!"

"But what is this?"

"It is a small device that serves to activate a magnetic shield..."

"Magnetic shield! What do you mean?"

"As soon as you trigger it, an invisible shield will protect you and everyone else by your side!"

"That's so cool! But how do I do it?"

"Just press this single button! But remember: use only in case of extreme precision, as the battery's charging capacity is small and, with that, you will have only two protections, understand?"

"Yes. But then, won't I be able to use it anymore?"

"Of course, yes! However, it will take a few hours for the battery to pick up a new charge, charging it with solar energy."

"Cool, I think we're going to make a good team, Allan!"

"So, boys, I just want to wish you a good trip right now; be careful and be very wise!"

"Thanks," the boys spoke at the same time.

"But why don't you go with us?"

"I can't, Samuel…I have several commitments to fulfill, which require a certain urgency…But I'm sure that you two will do very well…"

"Well, we already wasted a lot of time! I'm going to open the portal now, Zoorak."

"Yes…And again, good luck to you! I hope you return as soon as possible!"

Allan just waited for the alien friend to finish what he was saying to come over and give him a big hug. Then he took five steps forward and, more than quickly opened that magnificent lighted door that, surely, few would have the opportunity and the immense pleasure to contemplate. For him, that passage was not just a fantastic or magical thing, it was something even bigger: it was the entrance that gave access to his uncles, which he wanted so much to find, with this, to bring happiness and a smile back to his loved ones, grandparents.

As soon as he typed the desired date on the control screen, he looked back, called his faithful friend and finally they entered, giving Zoorak a goodbye and a big smile.

In a fraction of a second, as if in the blink of an eye, the boys arrived at a place that was nowhere near what they had left. The immense hills, with their forests, fauna, and rocks, had disappeared, finally giving way to a new environment.

Chapter XI
The Roman Empire

For more than a minute, Allan and Samuel stood there silently and still, watching everything. The feeling was that they were dreaming, but deep down; they knew that it was all very real. Only after a few moments, seeing that the portal was still open, did Samuel decide to break the silence:

"Allan, where are we? What was the location and date you typed on the screen?"

"Rome, Italy…Year 80 after Christ!"

"But where is the city?"

"We ended up in a rural area. Look around us…All of this is grape plantation!"

"My goodness! I'm a little worried now. Did we do well!"

"Don't worry, Samuel! Just as I will close the portal now, I will be able to open it at any time to leave!"

"Yes, all right…So let's go for a walk and see if we can find your uncle once and for all!"

"Look, Samuel, over there. It looks like a road made of stones.

"Let's find out!"

"Yes, but first I will choose a good bunch of grapes because I am very hungry! Want one too?"

"Not now, thank you! What I really want is to resolve this matter as quickly as possible."

"There, I already chose! Then let's go."

When they were approaching the trail, Allan noticed some movement in the distance and immediately shouted to his friend,

"Get down, Samuel! Come on, let's hide behind that rock!"

"But what is it? What is happening?"

"Look ahead, coming down the road…It's a huge Roman army with infantry and cavalry."

"Oh my! What will we do?" Samuel asked in distress.

"Let's be very quiet and wait for them to pass!"

"Did they see us? I'm scared to death!"

"Don't worry; I'm pretty sure they didn't see us!"

As soon as the legion approached, one of the soldiers, who was on the front line, began to gesture and shout as if he were giving an order to someone who, apparently, was on the way,

"Get out of the way, old woman! The emperor is in a hurry."

"Sorry, I was distracted, and I don't listen very well," said the frightened lady.

Not satisfied with that explanation, another soldier who was in the rear allowed the troops to go ahead, approached the elderly woman, punched her, and ran after his companions, laughing loudly.

"Coward! Come on, help her, Samuel."

"Yes, let's go!"

The boys quickly arrived and were soon raising, carefully, that poor old woman who was crying and lamenting the violence she had suffered.

"Are you okay? Why did he do it?"

"First, thank you so much for helping me! Well, I think I'm fine, except for exfoliations and this eye that must be black!"

"And it's really black," said Allan, brushing the hair off the old woman's forehead.

"As time gets better…But, continuing to answer your question, I can't tell you why he did it! One thing is certain, there are good and bad people everywhere in the world. My son, for example, serves in an army troop in a Roman province far to the north, and what I know is that everyone who knows him gives great praise to him as a person and as a soldier…"

"They seemed to be in a hurry…The emperor should be with them," deduced Allan.

"OH! Then that's it. At the time, I didn't even pay attention to what they had said. I think that, more and more, I am listening less. What is certain is that Emperor Titus Flavius should be in a hurry, as he cannot wait to open the Flavian amphitheater soon and appease the people of Rome…"

"I'm sorry, but I don't understand! I was away for a while and I don't know anything," argued Allan, trying in this way to get interesting information.

"Well, then I will tell you from the beginning…Last year, due to illness, the great emperor Vespasian died. In his place was the one you just saw passing by, Titus Flavius Vespasianus Augustus, his eldest son…Ironically, so far, he has not been very lucky in his government, despite his high competence. The eruption of Mount Vesuvius, for example, was a sad tragedy that will never be forgotten, because, in addition to the high mortality rate, it completely wiped out the cities of Pompeii and Herculaneum, significantly damaging Rome's trade. To make matters worse, some fires, seeming to be on purpose, happened here, precisely, or rather, 'coincidentally', on one of the days when Titus was out visiting one of those cities. Unlucky or not, the people, who were already distressed and frustrated, still had to live with the plague…"

"Plague?" Allan asked.

"Yes, an unknown disease, which recently appeared here, causing the death of several people…But, today, what is most commented here is that his own brother Domitian seems to be conspiring against his government! So I think that, for these reasons and, perhaps, others that interest him, he wants to open the amphitheater as soon as possible and, apparently, it must be today…To tell you the truth, I even wanted to go, because it is a colossal work and magnificent that began to be built in the government of its father. It will certainly be a party with many events and, from what people are saying, it will have a hundred days of attractions!"

"A hundred days!"

"Yes, that's right! But on second thought, I don't think I will. I hate gladiator fights, it's horrible and inhuman. The problem is that much of the population loves and…"

"Wow! And who are these gladiators?" Allan asked, very concerned.

"They are usually slaves, criminals, and also outsiders who appear here."

"Samuel, she is telling me that the Flavian amphitheater, which from what we have already studied is the Coliseum, will be opened today…To tell you the truth, I don't like any of this!!"

"But why not? It must be great."

"I'll explain later."

"What are you talking about?" The old lady asked, not understanding a word.

"Ahh! Nothing really! He just wanted to know what we were talking about…He's not a Roman. He came from a place very, very far from here, which is why he doesn't speak our language."

"Oh good! But who are you? And why do you wear these different clothes?"

"My name is Allan Smith, and this is my friend Samuel! I'm from the region, but I'm currently living at his house. There they have a habit and culture of wearing these types of clothes!"

"Yes. But what are you doing here?"

"In reality, I am looking for my uncle who also came from this distant place."

"Hmmm! I can't say for sure, but I think I saw him…To be more precise, I saw two, because they wore clothes like yours."

"Yes…They are! But one is my uncle and the other is…Well, never mind! But where did they go?"

"They followed this way, via Appia, toward the center of Rome," said the lady, pointing her index finger.

"So, let's go, Samuel. We will follow the emperor's army from afar."

"Wait…You can't go like this, dressed like that! Come on, my house is right there behind the grape plantation…There I have some clothes from my son when he was younger."

"Thanks, this will help a lot." Allan was happy with the old woman's kindness.

The three quickly reached the small house. They changed clothes and ate, drinking delicious grape juice, accompanied by bread that had recently been baked in a clay oven.

As soon as they said goodbye to the humble old lady, something in the corner of the kitchen caught Allan's attention.

"What is this doing here?"

"Ahh! I forgot to comment. One of those men you are looking for has dropped. I don't know what it is, but I kept it as a precaution."

"Look, Samuel, it's that bastard's weapon…The luck is that he dropped it, and it looks like it's discharged."

"It is a good thing that this Iron Fist Tiao had a 'rusty' aim, as your uncle Milton arrived here alive."

"At least one good thing, my friend."

"And what are we going to do with it, Allan?"

"Could you do me a favor?"

"Yes!"

"Bury it deep, where no one can find it, okay!"

"Rest assured; I'll do it!"

"One more thing…Where should I start looking for my uncle?…The city is gigantic!"

"Surely your uncle and that other one has already been captured. Foreigners here have no voice…Either they are in the slave market, or they must already be preparing to go into combat as gladiators!"

"That's what I feared…Come on, Samuel, because we don't have time to waste!"

"So, let's go!"

"Goodbye, my good lady. And thank you so much for everything," said Allan, hugging her.

"Go in peace and remember go straight down the road and in about twenty minutes you will get there."

***

The two boys finally set out for the long-awaited center of Rome. The road was perfect; the stones placed one by one were properly laid. Without a doubt, it was one of the most magnificent works made by the Romans at that time. Despite the good quality of the road, Samuel, who was anxious and couldn't wait to arrive, remembered one thing.

"Why don't we go flying? It will be much easier and faster."

"I don't think it's the time, my friend! The best thing is not to attract attention and get there very discreetly."

"You're right, Allan! The good thing is that we have the chance to see so many beautiful things along the way…And what I have noticed most is the large number of plantations of grapes and of olive trees!"

"It is true! The ancient peoples made many wines and olive oils."

"What's that up front, Allan? It looks like a bridge."

"It's an aqueduct!"

"Aque…What?"

"Aqueduct. It is a water piping system, used a lot in the past…Some were like that, very high. The goal is to bring water from distant locations to the city center, supplying public sources and the homes of the wealthiest."

"Gosh, it's amazing how fantastic the engineering of the past was!"

"And we haven't seen anything yet, or rather, we will see it now…Look ahead, it's already the city."

"My goodness, it's huge! I would never have imagined it was like that!"

"Well, let's go in very discreetly and remember keep your mouth shut."

As soon as they entered, the boys were increasingly impressed and admired the magnificent urban structure of Rome. On each street they entered, they saw several houses, shops, water sources, bridges, and dozens and dozens of people moving on foot or horseback. As soon as they arrived in the central area, they noticed that it was even more imposing because it contained the main buildings of that great empire.

Then, they stopped and stood there, for a few minutes, observing, in detail, the beautiful public buildings, theaters, gardens, arches of triumph, obelisks, and the immense temples dedicated to the many, many gods idolized at that time. Despite all the beauty, they also noticed the great difference in social classes, very common in any other great metropolis in the world. While the beggars, the sick, and the unemployed, dumped the rubbish, the most successful went to work or enjoyed their wealth, accompanied, in most cases, by their slaves.

Taking advantage of the round of some soldiers passing by Allan asked them,

"Please, where is the slave trade?"

"Over there, right after the two spas! From here to the Forum, you will probably take about fifteen minutes," one replied.

"Thanks! So, let's go, Samuel, we've already wasted too much time."

"What did you ask him?"

"I asked where the slave trade is."

"And what did he say?"

"Well, leaving here from the Forum, it will take us about fifteen minutes to arrive; he said it is right there in front, after two thermal baths."

"But what is the Forum and these thermal baths?" Samuel asked, scratching his head.

"You do not remember? We have already studied this in our history classes!"

"Yes…I mean, more or less!"

"Forum is this whole area where we are. It is a kind of gigantic square or, as you wish, it is the center of the Roman power. As you can see, this is where the main public buildings are located where everything important is decided…And the thermal bath is a place to bathe…It is very similar to the clubs of our time, with lots of water, physical exercises in the gym, massages, and other pleasures like games, reading, and lots of friends to chat with."

"Gee, I think I'm starting to like it here!"

"Yes, but not everything is a bed of roses! Well, let's pick up the pace."

Minutes later, they arrived in front of the slave trade. The place was sad, I could hear the crying of children, teenagers, and even adults.

As soon as they entered, the boys were shocked to see so much cruelty and inhumanity with the people who were there, in captivity, being sold as if they were mere commodities. Incredibly, at that moment there was no buyer. And it was not for less…With the opening of the Coliseum, which was about to start, everyone just thought about ensuring, in advance, their entrance to the long-awaited opening of the games. Anyway, after Allan looked closely at everyone, he saw that his uncle really wasn't there. He then approached his friend and said very quietly, "For sure, he must have been captured to be a gladiator…Only I didn't want to leave here knowing that these people would continue to be treated like animals!"

"I agree! But what are you thinking of doing?"

"Let's go. It is not good to call the attention of those two watchmen."

"So, let's go!"

Suddenly, Allan pointed to the cells and wished all of them to open as soon as possible. The slaves, seeing that the doors were no longer closed and nothing else was holding them, took off without leaving a child behind. The watchmen, who until then were more asleep than taking over woke up frightened, took up their weapons, and were again surprised by the power of the bracelet.

"What is it? Our swords have turned to clay!" said one of them.

"Let's get away from here too, this is something from some evil god," the other spoke.

Samuel was not content with joy and laughed and said to his friend, "Cool! Too bad we don't have time to go around freeing so many other people."

"Yes, it would be good! However, we came here for another purpose, and we cannot lose focus…The best thing to do now is to go straight to the Coliseum."

"But how are we going to get there?"

"Leave it to me!"

***

After a few minutes, they arrived in front of the long-awaited amphitheater. A magnificent construction that left everyone, without exception, amazed to see so much engineering sophistication.

At that time, thousands and thousands of people were there, eager to enter and see the inauguration party, the gladiatorial confrontations, and the animal struggles.

As soon as the gates opened, huge lines were organized by soldiers who had the purpose of avoiding riots and any other type of accident that could 'tarnish' that day so special for the emperor.

The boys, as smart as ever, were right in front, and as they approached the entrance, one of the porters stopped them and asked, "Wait, who are you with?"

Allan, who already expected that could happen, touched the bracelet, looked into the employee's eyes, and said, "Are you not recognizing me? Did you forget that we are related to the emperor?"

"A thousand apologies, boys! The imperial platform is right there…Have fun!"

"Thanks!"

"Gosh! I can't believe it…You hypnotized him!"

"Yes, I had no other choice!"

"Once we get in, where are we going to stay?"

"Anywhere, Samuel, as long as you can see the arena well."

"Wow! How beautiful it is inside…They had a great taste. Even marble they used! But what I liked most were those rows of bows…They are so cool!"

"I agree…And it will all go down in history!"

"See, Allan, it's already getting crowded. In a little while, no one else will fit…From what I noticed, there is the best spot and, if we don't hurry, we will have no place to sit."

"Sure! So, let's go just before someone gets there first and…Look at the podium, Samuel, it's the emperor…He just arrived!"

Immediately, everyone in the Coliseum stood and applauded the supreme leader, with great fervor. At that moment, it was very clear that the people loved and admired him, knowing that he would still do many other great things for Rome.

After a few seconds, Tito rose from his beautiful chair, made a greeting gesture, and then raised his right arm, making everyone silent to hear his opening speech and his order to start the show.

Anyway, after everything was authorized, the long-awaited parties began. There were so many attractions that the people could hardly blink, laugh, and always applaud. Even the richest and most powerful were fascinated. And it was not for nothing: never, in all of Rome's history, they had the opportunity to witness an event with such quality.

Suddenly, an even louder and euphoric scream echoed at once throughout the stands. The reason for all this was the gladiators who had just entered the arena in a row and stood in the center, side by side, to greet the emperor and the entire audience.

The boys, at that moment, were static. Especially Allan, who really wanted to identify his uncle before those fighters started to confront each other using knives, spears, swords, nets, tridents, and other things.

The problem is that they all held a shield and wore a helmet with face protection, making recognition completely impossible.

Finally, seeing the anxiety and expectation of his people, Titus Flavius got up again from his seat raised both arms, and said loudly,

"Let the fights begin!"

As agreed, each fighter already had his opponent, and as soon as they started fighting, Allan immediately made a deduction.

"Notice, Samuel, practically no fighter over there has my uncle's physical build and features, except for those two-up front!"

"Wow, I hadn't noticed! It really looks like him…And now, what are you going to do?"

Immediately, Allan pointed to the two fighters and wished that they would be uncomfortable with the helmets so that they could be thrown to the ground. It didn't take a few seconds; Samuel got up from his seat, put his hands on his head, and shouted out loud,

"See, Allan, they have no helmet and…oh my God! It's them! Your uncle Milton and the miserable Iron Fist Tiao."

"We finally found him!"

"But and now!"

"Samuel don't get out of here. I'll fly over there to save him!"

"Wait, it can be dangerous! There are several archers there, on duty."

"You are right, my friend, but I have to take that risk!"

The moment Allan was getting ready to go, Tiao, who already had experience with fights and murders, applied an unexpected maneuver to his rival, pulling his sword and one of his fingers. Unable to endure so much pain, Uncle Milton rolled to the floor, all bloodied, causing everyone in the stands to shout for his death.

Seeing Uncle Milton, the emperor, who had not yet authorized the execution, stood up again and asked everyone:

"Do you want him to die?"

Allan immediately looked at his bracelet and wished that his voice came out much higher than normal to be heard well. Then he filled his chest with air and shouted in a very high tone:

"NO…I do not want him to die!"

Titus, surprised by Allan's voice, looked at him and said:

"You scream out loud, I'm surprised! But why don't you want him to die!"

"Because he is my uncle and I like him very much…If you allow me, I want to go there and fight for his life!"

"But you are just a boy! I cannot authorize."

"Let me go and I will show everyone here that I know how to fight very well!"

The audience, who liked everything that was different, started shouting insistently to let him go. Seeing that he had no other choice, as he did not want to go against the people, the emperor raised his arm and said,

"Very well, I authorize you to fight…If my people want, I will answer. But I am not responsible for the life of this boy! Soldiers take it down there and take out the other gladiators. I want an exclusive fight!"

As soon as Allan stepped into the arena, he ran to his uncle and said, "Uncle Milton, hold on, I'll get you out of here as soon as possible!"

"I'm so happy to see you. But how did you get here?"

"Just like you!"

"My nephew, please don't fight him, it's suicide!"

"Don't worry, Uncle. I know what I'm doing!"

Then came the order for the combat to begin. Without wasting time, Allan put a finger on the bracelet and wished that his strength and agility would increase several times. Then he took his uncle's sword and shield and stood there, attentively, waiting for the opponent to approach. Without much delay, Iron Fist Tiao approached with wide eyes, and an ironic smile and then shouted out loud,

"I'll finish you in a minute, kid. Know that I never liked you!"

"What a coincidence, I also never liked you!"

"Cheeky, I will make you into pieces and then I will kill your uncle. Who knows, I will win my freedom!"

"You talk too much and…"

Tiao barely waited for Allan to finish speaking and started off with all the ferocity. At first, he thought it would be easy, but soon saw that the boy had something different, because his strength and agility were unusual. Allan, who until then only defended himself, started to counter-attack, leaving his rival quite nervous and disoriented. In a matter of minutes, the much-feared killer had already lost his shield and gained several cuts across his body. Seeing, then, that he was being completely humiliated by a boy, he decided, again, to charge, with all his fury, and once again he was surprised, losing his sword at last.

"Surrender, bastard!"

Pretending to be submissive, the colonel's henchman knelt, sneaked a piece of sand on the floor, and hurled it in his opponent's eyes. Realizing that his plan had worked, Iron Fist Tiao stood up quickly and pushed his opponent with much hatred, causing him to lose his sword and shield.

"Get up, damn kid, fight me unarmed!" Allan, who had barely risen and much less wiped his eyes, was surprised once again with a new push. And as soon as he was going to take another one, he sensed the scoundrel approaching and applied a nice judo blow, sending him far away.

Immediately the audience, which was already on its feet, began to applaud and demand the death of the loser. Seeing that his people were happy and euphoric, the emperor raised both arms and said,

"Boy, I was impressed by your fighting style. Your opponent seems to have broken one of his legs and is unable to get up…Well, if you kill him, I will give your uncle freedom!"

"No, I will never do that!"

"Nobody refuses an order from me. You will pay dearly for it! Soldiers, have one of the animals released."

Looking like magic, a huge cage came from the underground of the arena in a kind of elevator. Inside it was a large tiger that, when released, attacked the first person it saw standing: Allan. At that moment, the boy raised his arm, held the bracelet firmly with the other hand, and wished his strength and agility would improve even more. Then, with a beautiful and gigantic leap, he freed himself from the deadly attack of the animal that was just a few centimeters away to grab him.

The animal, seeing that it had lost its prey, decided to go toward Uncle Milton, attracted by the strong smell of blood.

Allan, like lightning, picked up a net, forgotten by one of the gladiators, and hurled it at the beast. Then he joined the two ends and, with superhuman strength, dragged it and left it in a corner of the arena temporarily trapped.

Although the public went wild, shouting and applauding a lot, the emperor was not at all satisfied; because he wanted the boy had die. Then he called two soldiers who were close to him and said to them:

"Arrest him immediately…I want him to know that nobody here disobeys me!"

In a matter of minutes, a large door opened in the arena and two chariots entered, a kind of mini carriage containing two horses, adapted exclusively for battles. As soon as they were approaching, Allan quickly pointed to the vehicles and wished the wheels to lock, causing the soldiers who were there to fall violently to the ground.

"What happened to them, my nephew? Did they die?"

"Calm down, Uncle…I already checked them, and they just passed out. Come on, I'll help you get on one of those chariots."

"But for what? We can't get out of here!"

More than quickly, Allan pointed to Samuel in the stands and made him float up to the arena. As soon as he arrived, Uncle Milton, who was completely amazed, said,

"What is this…? Is it magic?"

"I'll explain later, Uncle!"

At that moment, a lady who was in a sector of the grandstand, destined for the rich, took off an expensive gold necklace with diamonds and hurled it toward Allan, saying, "Take it; I was very surprised by everything, not to mention that you remember my late son a lot!"

"Thank you…I appreciate it!"

"And now, what are we going to do?" Samuel asked all concerned.

"Get on that chariot; I'll go on this one with my uncle! And, on second thought, I think I'll take the scoundrel with us. I won't leave him suffering here!"

"I don't know if it's a good idea, my nephew! But it's up to you!"

As soon as Allan thought of looking for him, the huge tiger managed to free himself and threw himself fiercely on Tiao, instantly ending his life.

"May God forgive him of his crimes and so many other sins!" said Uncle Milton.

"Ready? So, let's fly out of here now!" As soon as Allan started to concentrate on looking at the bracelet, Titus Flavius ordered the archers to shoot all his arrows.

"Samuel, use your device now!"

"Oh yes! I'm glad you reminded me!" Immediately, a huge magnetic shield protected the two chariots, preventing them from being hit. The three flew away, victorious, hugely applauded by the entire audience who had never seen anything like it.

"Damn you!" the emperor muttered very quietly.

Minutes after they left the Coliseum, Samuel, showing great concern, asked:

"Allan, how's your uncle doing?"

"Not good! The blood keeps coming out and he's complaining about a lot of pain. I confess I'm very worried!"

"I am too! What are you planning to do?"

"Well, I was thinking that, before opening the portal, we should look for that lady that we met. Who knows, maybe she has some medicine that can help."

"Good idea. Let's hope!"

"Yes…But regardless, I would love to see her again to say goodbye."

"I agree, she was so nice and helpful!"

"How lucky, it seems that we are already close, see, ahead, the grape plantations."

"Really! Wow. Flying is much faster!"

"Without a doubt, Samuel! And look, right in the middle, it's her little house."

"Cool! So, let's go down."

As soon as they landed, the old woman opened the door because she heard the noise of horses. When she saw the boys, she said,

"What a pleasant surprise! I am happy that you came back and from what I see, you got what you wanted!"

"Thanks! It was a very difficult task, but we finally managed to find my uncle."

"And the other?" The lady asked, looking toward the chariots.

"Well, he was not very lucky! But life is like that…"

"By the gods, your uncle is bleeding a lot!"

"Yes…He had a serious accident! Can you help him?"

"Yes. Take him inside and wait for me for a while…I'll get clean water and get some herbs!"

The kind old lady quickly provided everything. With great care and with experience of a long life, she cleaned the wound enough to avoid infection. Then he bathed with some herbal remedies and bandaged the wounds.

Uncle Milton, who finally drank some delicious tea and ate some treats, got up and gave the lady a big hug saying,

"Thank you very much; I will never forget what you did for me!"

Even though the elderly woman did not understand a word, she understood the affection she had received. And finally, after everyone said goodbye, Allan ran to one of the chariots and came back with something in his hand.

"This is a gift for you!"

"For me? But what a beautiful necklace, it must have cost a lot of money and…No, I can't accept it!"

"Stay, I insist! With it, you can expand your business and have an even better life."

"Very well, thank you! Today was a very special day for me. I met you and I also received great news, just now, that my son is returning…It seems that he will leave the army to work with me here at the plantation. I think you guys brought me luck!"

"That's good! I hope you have a lot of joy with him here and…Thanks for everything!"

"You're welcome…goodbye!" Quickly, the three picked up the chariots and left for a quiet and hidden place. Uncle Milton, who was no longer in pain at the time, questioned,

"How did you get those powers and how did you locate me?"

"Good, Uncle…I will explain it to you as soon as possible! But now we must try to save Uncle Alberto."

Chapter XII
The Inca Empire

As soon as Allan finished speaking, he immediately opened the portal, typing in the desired date, and, more than quickly, they entered it with the chariots, leaving once and for all that incredible and fantastic city that was the capital of the Roman Empire.

It didn't take even a few seconds and they found themselves in a completely different place. It was a great valley with waterfalls in the distance, and mountains everywhere, almost all with terraces that were kind of big steps made by the natives for planting purposes. In the flatter area, most of the plantations were concentrated, such as corn, potatoes, cassava, and cotton, irrigated by an ingenious system. In another part, you could see small houses and pastures for the llamas. The climate was very good; however, because they are in an area of the Andes, almost 3000 meters above sea level, the simple act of breathing became more difficult because of the thin air.

After about five minutes of just admiring that lush landscape, Samuel decided to ask,

"Where is this city?"

"Cusco must stay close by; the portal does not miss! Well, then the way is for me to go to those houses and ask the countryside where it is!"

"Take care, my nephew, if anything happens wave to us!"

"Do you want me to go with you?"

"You can leave it, Samuel, stay here with my uncle and take care of the horses."

"Okay...Good luck!"

As soon as Allan entered the small village, he saw an elderly couple sitting on small logs threshing some ears of corn. Around him, several children ran everywhere, others were entertained with their pets and some of them helped the elderly.

"Good morning," said Allan, showing a lot of politeness.

At that moment, everyone stopped doing what they were doing, and they watched that boy who was very different from the others with whom they lived. Only after a few seconds did you reply,

"Good morning, what do you want?"

"I would like to know where Cusco is, can you inform me?"

"Yes. Cusco is our capital, where our sovereign, the Inca Pachacuti…is in that direction behind those great mountains," said the old man, chewing a coca leaf.

"And how do I get there? Is there a road?"

"Yes. As it is a sacred area for all our people, the emperor ordered a good road made of stones! Now, if you prefer, you can go walking along the riverbank."

"Thanks!"

"But be very careful! They are taking outsiders to be sacrificed at the big party that will take place today, in honor of the Sun God."

"Yes, I will! And did you happen to see…"

At that moment, Allan stopped his question when he noticed that the other members of the village had arrived from their harvests and were there, observing with much curiosity his dress, which was still from the time of Rome.

"Do not worry. Everyone here is friends and will not hurt you! But what were you really going to ask?" The elder said.

"Did you or any of you see a young man in a different outfit and with light hair?"

"Yes," replied a girl holding a huge basket with llama wool to weave.

"Really!"

"No…I mean, I heard."

"Heard what?"

"Today, when I was in the city, everyone there only commented on two gods who came out of a huge and very bright door, there in the main square, in front of the palace…As for the priests, they say that they came out of a small star and, for this; they will be honored today at the big party…I also heard that one of them has light hair!"

"And where are they now, do you know?"

"Yes, they are staying in the great temple of the sun!"

"Thanks for the info!"

"Wait, don't go without food, the path is long," said the old man.

"Don't worry, I'm not too hungry."

"No way, I insist! Bring him something to eat!"

Then the girl ran quickly to one of the houses and brought boiled white corn, milk, and roasted fish with manioc. Seeing the education of those people, Allan gladly accepted and went to enjoy that delicious meal. As soon as he finished, he thanked them and asked,

"Will all those ears that you just brought from the plantations be threshed?"

"Yes," replied the girl.

"So, if I may, I want to do something in return for the immense kindness I received from you!"

"It is what it is?" The elder asked curiously.

Calmly, Allan looked at his bracelet and pointed to two things.

"By the Sun God! Look at what he did! All ears were threshed in seconds and the wool I brought was transformed into a beautiful fabric," said the girl with her hands on her head, not believing what she had just seen.

Soon everyone knelt and the elder spoke, raising his arms up,

"He is also a god and has come to bless our village!"

"I don't want to be called a god, just a friend! Well, I think it's time to go because I really want to find that one with the light hair…Thanks again!"

Upon returning, he immediately told his friend and uncle what he had just learned.

"Thank goodness, my brother is still alive, and he was not caught to be a slave! So, let's go there now."

"Calm down, Mr. Milton! Your brother and that scoundrel came out of the portal and were seen as gods! Now, nothing prevents us, when we get there in Cusco, that they confuse us as enemies."

"Yes, you're right, Samuel!"

"Wait, I just had an excellent idea…As we already knew and we also just confirmed the Incas, when they cannot explain certain events, analyze it as something supernatural, a mystical thing, interference from the gods, and…"

"Yes, we already understand nephew, but so what!"

"Well, the idea is to get there in the central square, flying with the chariots and also doing some special effects…What do you think?"

"Great."

***

They then left for Cusco with all their courage. Samuel also asked his friend to deviate a little from the path so that they could get to know the famous Lake Titicaca. Not wanting to upset him and knowing that it was a very touristic place, Allan did not think twice about flying over all that immensity of water.

"Wow, how cool, I had never seen such a big lake in my life! You see, it has small floating islands and houses."

"Well observed, my friend! I remember that I once read about these artificial islands. They are made with vegetation called Tule, a kind of reed. Even boats are made this way!"

"Since you talked about boats, Allan, look at the boat ahead. There are several small children disembarking and going to meet the warriors!"

"Yes, Uncle Milton! Those men seem to be from the emperor's army…And look, it seems like they're taking the children! I suspect that…"

"Do you think they will be sacrificed!" asked Samuel, his eyes wide.

"Well, I don't know what it is. So, the best thing to do is not to interfere. What I do know is that we should already go to Cusco, what do you think?"

"Yes," answered the uncle and the friend together.

They then proceeded to the famous capital of the Incas. On the way, flying over countless valleys and mountains, the three watched in awe, at the enormous number of roads, bridges, and walls made by that people. But only when they approached the city and saw countless houses, streets, squares, temples, and a magnificent palace did they really understand the fame and greatness of that civilization.

As soon as they flew over the central square, Allan put his index finger on the bracelet and wished that the two chariots radiated bright and colorful beams of light so that the sun would not overshadow the beautiful effect of the lighting.

Immediately, all the people in the immediate vicinity stopped what they were doing and kept pointing up, shouting over and over that it could be some deity.

As soon as they landed, several people, including nobles and priests, made a circle around the visitors, admired and impressed by all that luminosity and by the horses, which were animals that they had never seen before. Allan, to impress even more, touched the bracelet again and floated over everyone who was there.

Only after a few seconds, seeing that his plan had worked, did he ask, "Where can I find the god with light hair?" Before having the answer, the emperor left his palace and asked everyone to be silent.

Then, very nervous and afraid of that new event, he asked,

"Who are you and where did you come from?"

Quickly, a boy of an appearance different from that of the Incas ran toward the king and said to him,

"The god with the light hair asked to tell him that they are gods of good and that they came from the same place as him!"

Allan, who was still floating, looked to the side and saw his uncle approaching. In a gesture of joy, he shouted, smiling,

"It's him, it's Uncle Alberto!"

At that moment there was only laughter, but after so many hugs, the questions came,

"I'm so happy to see you! But how did you manage to find me? How did you get here? And what powers are these?"

"Don't ask me anything, my brother; the boys are the ones that know everything! They promised me that later they would tell me everything!"

"Okay…Come, I'm going to introduce you to the emperor."

"But how can you communicate with him, Uncle?"

"I have an interpreter, it's that boy over there at the palace door…He certainly knows that we are going to need him!"

"Maybe not, my brother…Your nephew, with all these powers, can understand any language!"

"Wow! You really are looking for like real gods…Well, come on then."

As soon as they approached the sovereign, everyone made a gesture of greeting, and then Allan addressed him,

"Nice to meet you, lord emperor! I speak on behalf of everyone here and I want you to be aware that we have come in peace."

"The god with light hair had already told me about you! It is a pleasure to have you here on the day of the feast of the sun!"

"Thanks!"

"However, I am very sad and nervous about what happened!"

"What happened?"

"The Evil God has kidnapped my son…"

"Evil God!"

"Yes, that other one who also came out of the little star! If you can do anything, I will be immensely grateful."

"Well, as we arrived now, the ideal is to know more details about this event!"

"Yes, I understand…Talk to the god with the light hair and he will explain everything to you!"

"Okay, we'll have a meeting now, and in a little while, I'll tell you what we decide!"

"Thank you, young God!"

Immediately, Allan called his group and went to talk at the temple of the Sun God, which seemed to be a more peaceful and reserved place.

"Uncle Alberto, what did Chico the Ambusher do to his son?"

"Well, when we arrived here, through a very bright portal, the people thought that we were real gods. With that, from the beginning, we were treated with the greatest privilege, respect, and admiration…Chico even forgot that he wanted to kill me. He was so dazzled by the power and wealth of the city that he began to play the role of a good man, or rather, a kind god so that he could take advantage of everything…But it was only to know that there was a fortune in gold there Machu Picchu, which revealed his great ambition and wickedness…With one shot, he killed one of the priests to show his power. Then he placed the gun on the head of Tupac Yupanqui, who is the son and heir to the throne, pressing him to show the way to the famous sacred city of the Incas…And there is more, a small indigenous tribe, contrary to the Pachacuti government, and also several rebels here in the city left with them showing total submission to Chico the Ambusher."

"It seems that the situation is not good! The emperor really has plenty of reasons to be sad!"

"Yes, my nephew, and it all happened, precisely, now when I was warning the bad character and the greed of the then 'Evil God'."

"Well, at least you did your part. From what I've noticed, everyone here admires you a lot, my brother!"

"Yes, you've already paid attention that they treat me like the god of light hair, right? Well, since the moment I arrived here, I tried to show good character and even taught them new planting techniques, some food recipes, medicines based on medicinal plants, and some mathematical calculations..."

"Whoa, you're very smart," said Samuel.

"Not really! Just a few experiences of my day-to-day life on the farm!"

"Uncle, tell me a little bit about the emperor and how he rules this whole empire?"

"Well, Allan, this subject is better left to my interpreter here, as he has been in this place longer than I have!"

"As far as I know, Emperor Pachacuti has been in power for many years. From the beginning, he was always seen as an excellent warrior and a great audacious general...And, besides, a great administrator, planner, philosopher, and a very charismatic person. For this reason, the people consider him as a kind of deity, and many here call him 'the son of the sun'...Here in Cusco, as far as I know, he has implemented a solid and effective administrative structure and, with this, he has become more and more powerful, thus being able to expand his empire with conquests of enemy cities and tribes. The conquered lands are completely under his control, giving him every right to charge extremely high taxes and free labor for any construction or renovations throughout the empire."

"It seems he has a strong and powerful army," said Uncle Milton.

"Yes! But most of the time Pachacuti doesn't even have to use force. When he wants land, he sends a messenger to the region and offers the leader advantages of wealth and education for the whole family, if he joins and submits himself to the empire." concluded the boy.

"Dang! How smart he is," exclaimed Samuel.

Allan understood everything, but something that had nothing to do with the conversation caught his attention,

"How did you learn our language?"

"I learned it from my father! He taught me when I was still a child...There in my tribe, everyone speaks his language fluently."

"But this makes no sense at all! In the year that we are no one from this region or from any other around here would be able to do such a thing! Where is your tribe?"

"I don't know exactly where it is. But, for sure, it is very far from the lands of Pachacuti."

"And how did you end up in this place?" Allan insisted.

"Well, as far as I remember, it was a day when my father was sick and couldn't go out hunting…So I asked him to give me the permission to go in his place. I really wanted to show everyone in my tribe that I was already a man and prove my talent with the bow and arrow. As soon as I got the authorization, I painted my face, asked for protection from the god Tupa and I went into the forest…The hours passed, and I was failing. Shamed to return with nothing, I did something I could never have done I entered an area forbidden by my tribe, hoping to get some game. I was very afraid because that place has always been known as a haunted place, a place of beasts never seen before. When I decided to leave, I came across a gigantic animal that started chasing me…In despair…I ran aimlessly and ended up passing by a light that appeared in front of me. I don't know how I got here in the Cusco region. I cried a lot and when they found me, I was made a slave for forced labor. Over time I learned their language, and when they saw that I knew Tupi Guarani and some other languages, they decided to put me in an interpreter position to serve the emperor."

"I already know where you came from and who you are! You can be sure, your father will be immensely happy when he sees you again, Uirapuru!"

"But how do you know my name?"

"Not only yours, but that of your two sisters: Jaci and Irani…And also, that of your father, Mr. Acaua!"

"By Tupa, I'm not even believing it!"

"I am the one who is not believing! We've been together for some time, and I didn't even suspect anything," said Uncle Alberto.

Finally, everyone approached and hugged the young Indian who, at that moment, cried a lot with emotion.

Soon after, voices and weeping from children coming from outside the temple caught the attention of everyone there.

"Wow, come and see…It's those little children from Lake Titicaca! Those warriors brought them here," said Uncle Milton.

"Unfortunately, they will all be sacrificed today on the feast of the Sun God," said Uirapuru.

Suddenly, Allan, looking very worried, left stepping with firm steps, saying,

"I will immediately go and talk to the emperor…I have a proposal to make to him!"

"Wait, my nephew! Tell us what you are up to!" asked Uncle Alberto.

"I will say that I will help him, but on one condition!"

"So, I'll go along, because before you got here, he had already asked me the same thing…Surely, whatever you agree, you can count on me," Alberto said.

Finally, everyone wanted to go too and, more than quickly, they left together toward the palace. As soon as they arrived, Allan immediately said to Pachacuti:

"Mr. Emperor, I, on behalf of everyone here, would like to tell you that we decided to go to Machu Picchu to rescue your son."

"OH! Thank you very much, Child God!"

"But only on one condition…"

"And what is it? Tell me. If it is within my reach!"

"We will bring him back if he spares the life of all those children who will be sacrificed and also gives this boy his freedom!"

"The young interpreter's freedom is fine. But the little children I don't know…The Sun God may revolt!"

"I can talk to him! I'll tell him it's for a good cause."

"All right, Child God! Bring my son back and you will have everything you want!"

***

As soon as they left the palace, Allan told everything he had talked about and then concluded:

"Nobody here has the obligation to go with me…If you prefer, you can stay, and I'll go alone."

"I want to go too!" they all said at the same time.

"Uncle Milton, I'd rather you stay, because your hand must not be very good yet!"

"Yeah…It really does hurt a bit!"

"Milton, so far I haven't asked you what happened to you when we entered that portal…And also how did you get this injury?"

"We have many things to share, my brother…But thank God, we are alive!"

"Uncle Alberto, you should stay too! It will be great to keep each other company."

"But I promised I would help!"

"Rest assured; I will tell Pachacuti that you two will stay in the temple to talk with the Sun God about the children."

"Oh, if that's the case, then fine. The problem is that we will be worried about you!"

"You don't have to worry, Alberto, they know how to handle themselves better than us!" said Uncle Milton.

"Okay, but please be careful!" Quickly the boys went to prepare the chariots. And when they were about to leave, the emperor approached and told them:

"I am also sending part of my army there…I just hadn't done it before; for fear that the Evil God might kill my son…But once you save him, nothing will stop us from taking back Machu Picchu, which has always been and always will be our sacred 'home'."

"Okay, as soon as we achieve our goal, I will send a signal in the sky, alerting those that everything is under control."

"Perfect! I will then order my warriors to stay hidden in the woods waiting for your command."

Finally, after everything was discussed and arranged, they all left for that rich and very mysterious city.

The boys preferred not to go with the army. They knew that if they flew with the chariots, they would arrive much faster to solve that embarrassing and very dangerous problem. Allan, who was with the young Indian, asked him,

"How well do you know the route Uirapuru?"

"Yes, I've been there a few times."

"And what is the city like?"

"Well, Machu Picchu is at a very high point in the Andes Mountain Range…To get there by walking, requires good physical preparation, because we must face forests, steep climbs and some stairs; not to mention the dangers with wild animals and huge cliffs! Because it is an area of difficult access and because it has a nearby river, they chose it to build the city that would be the impeacher's refuge in case of an attack. Everything was very well elaborated. The urban area, where the royal residence is located, has streets, houses, squares, temples, water fountains and several other constructions…The agricultural area has several terraces for planting and food storage enclosures."

"I have heard that there are some legends and mysteries about its development…What do you have to tell us?"

"That's right! Most of their constructions took rigorous astronomical criteria…Some had their alignment so perfect that it coincides with sunrise and sunset depending on the time of year…What is more intriguing is how they managed to transport huge stones, used in the various works, without having appropriate carts and animals. And that, not to mention how they carved and fit them, using only rudimentary tools."

"Gee, did they have any help?" Samuel asked on the other chariot.

"This they never commented, and it is the great mystery…They only say that a great effort was required of thousands of slaves and, moreover, the blessing and protection of the supreme god Viracocha who, for them, is the creator of this world! But once an old priest, who was very sick and kind of delirious, said that Machu Picchu, when it was being built, had help from intelligent beings coming from the stars!"

"Alien!" exclaimed Samuel.

"Yes. But we will never know, because the old man died days later…One thing is certain; one day the truth always comes out and…Look, up there on that mountain, it's it!"

For a few moments, everyone remained in silence admiring the imposing city. However, not everything there was beautiful to admire.

"You see, there are warriors almost everywhere, mainly there, at the entrance and also in the central courtyard."

"That's right, Allan! And now how are we going to get down without being seen?"

"Stay calm, Samuel!" said the young Indian. "I know a secret passage on the other side; we just have to find a safe place to leave the chariots."

"There seems to be a good place!"

"Yes, Allan, and that's exactly where the entrance is! See that big pointy rock on the mountainside? Well, it's below it!"

"And how did you find out about this?" Samuel asked all curious.

"The last time I was here, Emperor Pachacuti was doing an escape training, in case of any unforeseen event…And, as I have always been trustworthy, he allowed my presence."

"And where will we get out?" Allan asked.

"In a small warehouse that is right next to the royal residence…It's quiet, let's go!"

As they approached the entrance, Samuel stopped the body, got thoughtful, and then said,

"Wow, it's a tunnel and it's very dark! How will we see in there?"

Allan, seeing his friend's concern, caught three dry branches, pointed at them, and immediately lit them to use as torches.

"Nice," said Uirapuru.

With the flame, they were encouraged even more and walked for a long time on that underground path, until they came across a staircase made of wood, which gave access to a small passage closed by a stone lid. Without wasting much time, they went up and hid inside the small warehouse. The idea was to be very quiet for a while, analyzing the movement and the conversations that came from outside.

"Oh my God! I'm hearing steps coming here," said Samuel frightened.

Suddenly, a warrior with his face all painted and, with a knife in one of his hands, entered through the small door with the intention of catching some food. When he saw the boys, he put himself in an attack position and, very suspiciously, he asked them,

"Who are you and what are you doing here?"

Barely finished asking, he closed his eyes and fell to the ground in a deep sleep.

"What happened to him?" The young Indian asked.

"I had to make him sleep…Come on; let's drag him to the corner."

"Thanks to Tupa you have these powers! But now, what are we going to do? From what I can see from the door, the courtyard is still full."

"I have an idea. See those two huge blocks of stone up ahead? Well, look what's going to happen!"

"My goodness, they are floating," exclaimed Samuel.

"Now I'll throw them over that wall and let them roll down the mountain!"

Immediately, when they heard that loud noise, all the warriors ran down part of the mountain to see what had happened.

"You are a genius, my friend. Even more with this bracelet! The good thing is that our other friend here brought his bow and arrows to ensure as well," Samuel spoke.

"Yes, we might need to, right? Well, do you see this stone wall over here? So, the emperor's house is just behind…Come on, there's an entrance up ahead," explained the young Indian.

So, they ran as fast as possible. As soon as they entered, they came across two armed guards with spears that certainly were not for talk.

"Where do you think you are going?" One of them asked.

"We came to talk with your boss and…"

Uirapuru hadn't even finished responding and the big guys came with the weapons, ready to attack. Immediately, Allan raised his hand and transformed the spears into dozens of pieces. Seeing that they were not intimidated, he transformed the two guards into stone statues.

"My goodness! I almost died of fright! But what about now, will they stay like this forever?"

"No! Only until tomorrow! Stay calm, Samuel, so far everything is going very well!"

Unfortunately, for the bad luck of the boys, a third man, who was close to a small tree and who had witnessed everything, approached silently, behind the young invaders and hit, violently with some wood, the head of one of the boys, who he thought was the most powerful. Then he pointed the spear at the others and told them, "You are all under arrest, you are not welcome here!"

"My God, what have you done to my friend? He can't have died!"

"I'm sure Tupa won't take him, Samuel, because he is our only hope of getting out of here alive!"

An hour later, having gone through so much anguish, the two boys raised their hands and let out a cry of happiness at the same time,

"Hooray! He has opened his eyes, and he is moving!"

"I'm glad you're a 'hardhead'!"

"Stop joking, buddy, and tell me…Ouch, uh…Where are we?"

"I can see that your head is still hurting and the worse we are locked in an improvised cell, inside the royal residence…And look who is with us, sitting there in the corner!"

"Hmm…Who is he?"

"Uirapuru said that he is Tupac Yupanqui, son of the emperor."

"Good, at least we found him alive! Well, just give me a few more minutes to see if this pain gets better, and then we can think of a way out of here."

Suddenly, Colonel Faustino's henchman arrived in front of the cell door, laughed, and spoke loudly,

"Ahh! I see the old man's grandson is awake! What a shame, I really wanted you to die!"

"This taste, I won't give it to you so soon!"

"As always petulant…But tell me, how did you end up in this region?"

"We came in the same way as you and my uncle! And since you touched on it, I want to propose two things to you!"

"I don't think you're in a position to propose anything to me," replied the bandit, laughing more.

"Do you want to hear me or not?"

"Spit it out, brat!"

"As I told you, there are two proposals. The first is if you are interested in coming back with us to our world?"

"You can only be mad! Go back and be a Colonel's employee again? And run the risk of being arrested one day?"

"Well, if you didn't like it, then what do you think of us going back to Cusco…If you set us free, the emperor, with a request from me and my uncle, will give you jewels and land!"

"Do you think I'm dumb? First, he may as well have me killed, and second, I already have all that. Here I have nothing missing…I own the city; I have enough gold, jewelry, and land to plant, slaves and warriors that will gradually help me conquer other cities to create an empire…Only then will we become strong enough to conquer the capital Cusco."

"You are insane!"

"You're the one who must be delirious with the bump on the head! Well, I'll leave them a little. I will go to the warehouse to get a drink because I can't stand to be without the 'damned thing'. Stay very still!"

As soon as he saw that they were alone, Allan looked at the bracelet, raised both hands forward, and turned the cell door into smoke.

"Cool, let's get out of here," said Samuel all happy.

"Wait just a minute! I'm going over there at the scoundrel's table to get my bow and arrows."

As soon as everyone left the royal residence, they ran into Chico the Ambusher, returning from the warehouse with a pitcher of clay.

Amazed to see the prisoners released, he dropped the object, immediately drew his revolver, and fired the last two bullets in vain.

"Damn! I've never missed a shot in my life that close!"

"You perhaps wouldn't miss, but have you ever heard of a magnetic shield?" Samuel said grinning.

"Shield or not, now you'll see what I sharpened today and it's cutting like a razor!"

Allan, seeing that knife, raised his hand quickly and in a matter of seconds turned it to dust. Then, he pointed to a huge rock and made it fly in flames like a meteor.

"What kind of magic is that? You want to intimidate me, so I will do the same. I will now call my warriors!"

"Give it up, Chico! Your men, at this moment, must already be in confrontation with the immense army of Pachacuti."

"Oh! So, that stone with fire was a sign!"

"Yes. But, if you want, I can still help you!"

"Never, I'd rather die," the colonel's henchman spoke and opened some kind of cage.

"My God, what's in there?" Samuel asked worried.

"Have fun…" Chico ironized, running toward the temple.

For a few seconds that seemed like an eternity, they stood there, immobile and afraid, wondering which creature could get out of that door.

Suddenly, to everyone's fear, a huge jaguar roared and showed all its ferocity with immense claws and fangs.

For being closer to that door and for not having the slightest chance to run, Pachacuti's son was a sure target. But, as soon as the great jaguar, so known by the Incas, attacked and showed that it would give its fatal bite, it was killed, instantly, by a sharp arrow in the neck.

"Thank goodness you saved him!" Samuel was thrilled.

"Uirapuru, this time you have shown that you are really a man and that you know how to handle the bow and arrow very well…I am happy to have a friend like that! You can be sure, your father will be proud when he hears of your great heroic act," said Allan, giving him a hug.

"Thanks," replied the young Indian, moved and with eyes full of tears.

"Look, the Evil God is stealing the sacred statue of the Sun God!" said Tupac Yupanqui.

"I don't know what he said, but from here I can see the scoundrel carrying a statue all of gold," observed, too, Samuel.

More than fast, Chico the Ambusher ran like crazy through those dangerous mountains. Finally, when he saw a huge cliff, he stopped and stood there, analyzing where to go down. However, when he saw Allan approaching flying, he momentarily placed the statue on the ground, took a stone, and threw it at the boy with the intention of killing him.

"Give it up, Chico; you won't be able to hit me! Why don't you want me to help you?"

Without wanting to give a single word, the bandit took another much bigger stone and, as soon as he was going to throw it, he stumbled on the so valuable golden object, completely losing his balance. Having nowhere to hold it, he rolled all over the cliff and met a dry and pointed trunk that sealed its fate.

"My goodness, he's all perforated! What a horrible death! I hope God has mercy on your soul," said Allan and, returning to his friends, concluded, "This here belongs to your people, Tupac!"

"Thank you, Child God, for saving me and also for recovering the sacred statue!"

"Look…Pachacuti's army defeated the Evil God's accomplices and recovered the city again!" said Uirapuru.

"And speaking of an evil god, what happened to the scoundrel?"

"He died, Samuel…He went up there!"

"Up! He must have gone down."

"This mystery of life we will never know, my friend! Well, now we just must go back to the capital."

As soon as they landed with the chariots in the central square of Cusco, everyone, including the maximum leader, came to receive and greet the future heir to the throne.

"Thank the gods you are back," said Pachacuti, hugging his son strongly.

"They were incredible, my father! They defeated the god of evil and helped restore our holy city."

"Thank you, Child God…I will have an eternal debt with you!"

"Don't worry about it, emperor…Just keep what you promised…"

"Absolutely! I will spare the children's lives and, better, from now on, no child will be sacrificed! And, as I promised, the young interpreter is free."

"Thanks," replied Uirapuru smiling.

"Thank God, you have returned safe and sound!" said Uncle Milton, embracing them.

"I am also very happy that you have returned," commented Uncle Alberto, smiling.

"Let the feast of the Sun God begin…And you, gods who came from the stars, share with us our feast and celebration," says Pachacuti.

"Yes, we will stay for a while." Allan answered for everyone.

After staying for a long time in that extraordinary event, they approached, once again, the great leader to say goodbye.

"Well, it's time to go," said Allan, shaking the emperor's hand.

"What a pity, it was a pleasure to have you here!"

"The pleasure was all ours…And, for sure, we will come back one day for a little visit!"

"You and your people will always be welcome in our city…And, once again, thank you for everything, Child God!"

"You are welcome!"

"I would also like to thank you again for saving me! And I wish, from the bottom of my heart, to see you return one day," said Tupac Yupanqui.

"Wait, I want to give you a small souvenir of our city." Now it was Pachacuti who spoke, making a sign for two of his employees.

"No need to bother!"

"I insist, Child God…And I want to ask you a favor!"

"Yes, what is it?"

"I want you to open these bags only when you are at home."

"All right!"

Then, as soon as the two men put the bags tied on the horses, Allan opened the time portal, entered the intended date, and finally everyone entered through it, leaving, once again, the greatest Inca emperor of all time impressed and admired with the 'visitors of the stars'.

Chapter XIII
The Return to the Farm

Finally, everyone returned safe and sound to that mysterious place of departure.

"My God, I'm recognizing this damn place!

"The hills…Come on, we must get out of here as soon as possible!"

"Stay calm, Uncle Milton! The mysteries that exist here, Samuel and I have already unveiled…And, better, we have even made great friendships!"

"Friendships, here! Only if it was with some ghosts!" Uncle Milton was desperate, looking everywhere.

"Well, they're not really from this world."

"Not from this world!"

"It is true, Uncle! They are space travelers and have been here for many years with the sole purpose of studies and research…They chose this site because of the uranium that is used as fuel!"

"From what I can understand, they are aliens!" exclaimed Uncle Milton in admiration.

"I have understood everything!" said Uncle Alberto. "They are beings from another planet that certainly use several advanced technologies to scare any curious or adventurous person that comes around here…And, no doubt, our dear nephew here received some benefits from this intelligence."

"Yes, that's right, Uncle! Another time, I will tell you why!"

"Look, they're coming," observed Samuel.

"By Tupa! They look nothing like us!"

"No need to worry, Uirapuru, they are different, but they are polite, intelligent, and kind! Come, I will introduce them."

"Hello, Zoorak, Zurlly and Zuur…I'm glad to see you again!"

"We are also happy that you have returned!"

"Thanks, Zoorak. Without your help, we would not have achieved our goal!"

"No, Allan…The merits of this achievement are all yours!"

"Well, then I want to introduce my uncles, Alberto and Milton…And this here is our friend Uirapuru! He also went through the time portal on another occasion."

"Nice to meet you! This is my family, and we have other members there in our base…And, taking the opportunity, I want to apologize for having sent you to the past!"

"It's fine! We are aware that you have your reasons!" said Uncle Milton, making a face of pain.

"I see that you are feeling a lot of pain…And not for less, losing one of your fingers in a fight is not very pleasant!"

"But how do you know about this?" Uncle Milton asked intrigued.

"I can read your mind! Come, let's all go to our base. I think we can manage this hand."

"No need to be afraid, Uncle! There is a laboratory for studies of genetics, where they make clones of living beings, creation of organs, and regeneration of mutilated limbs!"

"You have a great memory, Allan! Let's go," said Zoorak.

Finally, after almost an hour, Uncle Milton left the cloning room laughing loud with happiness.

"Look, everyone! I know that they have a high knowledge of medicine here, but for me, this is a miracle…Thank you, my God, for intervening and healing my hand."

"I thank you, Zoorak, your family, and all your team for what you did for my uncle!"

"You don't have to mention it, Allan! What you did for my son is much greater than anything! As you already know, I will always be grateful!"

"Thank you. I hope to see you again on my next vacation!"

"We look forward to seeing you! Ahh…And every time you want to communicate with me, just wear your bracelet…We can communicate by telepathy."

"That's so cool! Did you hear that, Uirapuru? They can always have contact with each other," said Samuel all excited.

The young Indian didn't even seem to be there. He was so dazzled and amazed by that magnificent base that he didn't even pay attention to what his friend told him.

"Before you leave, I would like to ask you not to report anything you have seen here, can you promise?"

"Yes," all responded at the same time.

"Goodbye Zoorak…I will miss you!" Allan gave a hug to his new friend.

"And I too," Samuel added, repeating the same gesture.

Finally, they all got into the chariots and flew out of that place that, for them, was no longer mysterious, but a place of future adventures.

***

The sun was almost setting when they landed with the chariots in front of the main entrance of the colonel's farm. As soon as they walked in, they heard a very sad cry, coming near the barn and decided to find out who it could be. They walked in silence and soon realized that all the warriors were making a circle around a person who, at that moment, was distressed and disconsolate for having lost hope in their search.

"I don't know what will become of me from now on without my sons!"

"Don't be like that, Mr. Jorge! My son also disappeared some years ago and I never stopped believing that one day I will find him…I understand his pain, but never stop having faith!"

"You can believe it, Grandpa! And you too, Mr. Acaua…they're back here," shouted Allan thrilled.

Immediately, the two gentlemen turned and were paralyzed, for a few seconds, thinking that maybe it was a dream. And when they saw that it was all real, they ran and immediately went to embrace those they loved so much.

"My God, what joy I am feeling! Thanks for bringing them back," said Grandpa Jorge very excited, being affectionately embraced by his family.

"Thank you, oh my god, Tupa…There are times I dream daily about this day," said the old Indian in tears, hugging his beloved son strongly.

At that moment, all the warriors started to sing of happiness, and, with that, nobody paid attention to some noises coming from inside the barn.

Using a lever and a knife, found under a pile of hay, the colonel, taking advantage of that moment of euphoria outside, carefully tried to pull out a window that gave to the back of the small room. As soon as he made it, he climbed on a chair, jumped out, and stayed hidden, waiting for the right moment to disappear from there.

Tired of waiting so long, the colonel decided, then, to take someone hostage and go to the wagon to escape calmly. Seeing that Mr. Acaua was inattentive and that he would be a fundamental part of his plan, he ran as much as he could and took him as a prisoner.

"Quiet, Indian! Try anything and you will never see your son again, understand?"

"Please release my father," said Uirapuru crying.

"Let go of me! You are crazy!"

"Tell everyone to get out of the way or I will cut your neck with this knife."

"You heard him, get out of the way!"

As soon as they approached the wagon, the colonel, who was still mad with rage, continued shouting and threatening the native.

"It's your fault, you old fool Indian! If you hadn't meddled, everything would have worked out."

"Give up, coward! Your goons have died and now you have no one else to defend you," shouted Uncle Milton.

Allan, who was about to take an attitude, decentralized on seeing three men, looking like they had badges, approaching in total silence to listen to all that conversation.

"I repeat, if anyone tries anything, I will kill this man without mercy or pity, just like I did with everyone who tried to disrupt my plans."

"And why do you think you have the right to kill? Do you think this is right?" Allan asked smartly; already suspicious of who those people were back there.

"You really want to know, little boy? So, I'll tell you…But it's only because you're new in these parts and you don't know about my fame…"

"Yes, just say it, I'm curious!"

"Here *I am the law*. Even the sheriff and the politicians obey me…When I want something, like land, I threaten the owner and buy it cheaply…If I play the tough guy, I'll kill! To tell you the truth, I've already lost count of how many I've killed. The fun is to put them suffering before giving the fatal blow…"

"By cutting the person's neck, just like you did with the federal geologist?"

"Yes, it was my henchman, but I authorized it! Now it's very clear that you and that other brat, there on your side, have been here snooping and listening to my plans."

"And why don't you also tell me what you intended to do with my uncles who are here?"

"You know very well! I had them captured to blackmail your dear grandfather. And taking the opportunity, if you don't sell me the place by tomorrow, I will kill the old Indian and all of you!"

"Well, then you'd better explain everything you've just confessed to these guys who have been behind you for a long time!"

"What! Who are you?"

"First, release the boy and drop the knife…Thank you! As of today, I am the new sheriff of this region and these two are my assistants," replied the boy who was wearing a suit and tie and had a revolver in one of his hands.

"But what do you want here on my property?"

"Just work routine…Actually, we came to interrogate you!"

"Interrogate me! But why?"

"Before I accepted my transfer here, I already knew the problems of this region…"

"Problems?" The colonel asked, pretending to be a fool.

"Yes. That's exactly what you heard! To be clear, there are several occurrences of murders, kidnappings, beatings, blackmails, corruptions, robberies, and…Well, in most cases, your name is involved directly, or as a mastermind…The strange thing is that the former sheriff seemed to turn a blind eye, filing the cases or simply throwing them away…"

"But I have nothing to do with it!"

"Through the evidence I have, and everything we heard and witnessed minutes ago, you will have to come with us!"

Taking advantage that the old Indian was still close by, the colonel gave him a push, throwing him against the sheriff. Then, he quickly climbed on the wagon and drove off, desperate to get away from there.

Allan, who was attentive to everything, pointed to the exit of the farm closing the gate immediately.

"Dammit, who closed the damn gate…it looks like witchcraft!"

"Get off that wagon immediately, and don't try any more funny things, Colonel Faustino, because I won't hesitate to shoot!" the sheriff spoke already pointing the gun.

"No…Don't shoot, I surrender!"

"Put the cuffs on him! You are under arrest in the name of the law…You can take him."

"I hate everyone here, especially you, snoopy boy! You managed to deceive me and made me confess several things…You, damned demon," said the revolted colonel, staring at Allan.

As soon as they left, everyone there shouted euphoric with joy, vibrating intensely with hats, spears, and bows up. Uirapuru didn't want to waste any time; he ran slightly and hugged the old Indian once again.

"Father, no one will ever separate us again!"

"Yes, my son! I trust in Tupa!"

At this moment, Grandpa Jorge approached them both and told them, "Well, I think it's time for us all to go home…"

"But what about my daughters?"

"Leave them with me…Tomorrow I want all of you to come to the farm because I really want to have a party to celebrate the return of our children. Not to mention the prison of the scoundrel. Apparently, I think I'll be able to sell my crops now!"

"I thank you; we will go with great pleasure!"

"I am the one who has to thank you and also all the warriors of your village who have engaged in the search!"

"No need to thank, Mr. Jorge, after all, we all left satisfied! Well, see you tomorrow then."

After everyone said goodbye, they left the Colonel's farm, happy and satisfied with everything that had happened well and for the party arranged for the next day.

On the way home, Uncle Milton and Uncle Alberto explained to their father everything that had happened without forgetting any details. And as soon as they finished, Grandpa Jorge stared at his sons and told them,

"I believe everything you just reported…Only I know how much I suffered when I was in those hills! Until today I have nightmares, but I think I've gotten used to it! Well, the best thing to do is to keep it a secret and never reveal any of it to anyone!"

"Yes, Dad! So much so that we promised it," said Uncle Alberto.

"Who would have thought…? Those chariots the boys brought are genuinely from the ancient Roman Empire!"

"Yes!" replied Uncle Milton.

"And who would have thought, Father, that Allan would be the fundamental piece to unravel all those mysteries," completed Uncle Alberto.

"Funny, from the first moment I saw him, I don't know why, but I had an intuition that I was in front of a special boy and that he would certainly bring us many joys…Not to mention what the former owner of the place told me: that probably someone from my family would have an important mission in life…I see that we were both right!"

"For sure, your grandson is fantastic," said Uncle Milton.

***

When they arrived at the site, the first stars were already beginning to appear in the sky, accompanied by a bright full moon.

As soon as they put the animals away, the outside lights came on and, in the kitchen, door appeared the smiling and happy daughters of Mr. Acaua.

"Thanks to Tupa you found them! How nice, Miss Maria will be very happy," said Jaci.

"She is already waking up from her sleep…Surely, she will have a great surprise! But what about my father? Where is he?" Irani asked.

"He's fine! You can relax, your father will be here tomorrow, won't he, my sons?"

At that moment, nothing more was heard. Uncle Alberto and Uncle Milton, who barely knew the ladies were going to spend the night there, were paralyzed, admired, and enchanted by the beauty and sweetness of the two sisters.

"Eh…I think Cupid's little angel came by and shot some arrows," said Samuel smiling.

"But what a lack of attention to mine! Let me introduce my sons to you," Grandpa Jorge spoke, already suspicious of something.

Only after the presentations, did they come back to themselves a little, seeing the kind mother leave and approach with open arms.

"Oh, my good God, thank you for hearing my prayers!"

"Grandma Maria hugged her sons and cried with happiness."

"Let's all go inside and eat something…Then it's good to go to bed early to get up in a good mood for the party."

"Party? Which party?"

"This party that Grandpa just talked about, Grandma, is to celebrate the return of my uncles and the return of the…Well, never mind. Tomorrow Mr. Acaua will come with his friends and will make a good surprise for his daughters!"

"What surprise?" They both asked at the same time.

"Stop being curious and let's do what I said."

"Grandpa, wait just a few more minutes. Samuel and I will go quickly to the horses to get something we forgot!"

"Okay! But come back soon!"

"Come on, Samuel!"

"Yes, but what did we leave behind? I don't remember!"

"The gift bags that Emperor Pachacuti gave us…And he said that we should open them only when we were at home!"

"Yeah! I had forgotten…And what's inside?"

"I don't know, my friend. But we will know now." Moments later, the boys running through the house, hold those heavy bags.

"But what's gotten into you boys? It's like you have seen a ghost!"

"On the contrary, Grandma! Where are my uncles? We need to show something for them!"

"They're there in the living room with your grandfather…Wow, you are really in a hurry," said Grandma Maria smiling at the young women and at the same time stirring a big pot.

"Uncles, look at the emperor's gifts." Allan dumped the bags on a huge table.

"My goodness! There are several gold objects and many jewels," Uncle Milton exclaimed, his eyes wide open.

"And inside these other bags there is more." added Samuel.

"I don't think we should accept this fortune. Tomorrow, if you want, I will come back to Cusco and return this!" said Allan.

"No way, my nephew! I learned enough about the emperor to know that when someone doesn't accept his favor…Well, you can end up insulting him a quite much," said Uncle Alberto.

"He's right, Allan. After you have accepted a gift, it is very bad to return it."

"Yes, you both are right! Pachacuti could be extremely upset."

"Do you know what that means, guys? We will be able to pay all debts with the bank and sell the crops very calmly!" Uncle Milton looked very happy.

"Well, as only we know this secret, we will say that you, in that escape, found this treasure hidden and forgotten in those woods out there! Well, let's eat something and then sleep," Grandpa Jorge concluded.

***

The sun had barely risen, and everyone was already in the kitchen making a reinforced snack at breakfast.

As soon as they finished, the two brothers invited the ladies to get to know the place better and accompany them in some routine work.

Allan and Samuel wanted to go together to help in the services and, with this, they ended up making those tasks fun.

For Uncle Milton and Uncle Alberto, the day-to-day tasks such as milking cows, caring for animals, planting, collecting eggs, picking fruit and vegetables have never been carried out with such enthusiasm, because after all, they returned safe and sound and were completely in love.

"Look, Allan, your uncle Alberto always stays close to Jaci; already your uncle Milton talks more with Irani."

"Yeah, I have! I like to see them like this, happy. I hope everything works out."

"Allan, what do you say we go to the kitchen now, help your grandma with the party setup?" Uncle Milton asked when he finished his duties.

"Cool, I want to help too!" said Samuel thrilled.

Finally, after they made all the food, they immediately provided two large tables and put them under a huge mango tree. As soon as they lined them, they put on sweets, pies, cakes, cheeses, breads, popcorn, boiled corn, and several meats accompanied by potatoes and cassava.

Grandpa Jorge did not forget his guitar and, looking like he had arranged it, he started playing the first song, just when the guests showed up at the entrance of the farm bringing some musical instruments and several typical foods from the tribe.

"Look, they've arrived and they're coming in…Good!"

Jaci and Irani, who had just put their last refreshments on the tables, looked back and had a happy surprise when they saw their brother, missing for so long, approaching to give them a hug.

"Uirapuru! You are alive! My god Tupa, tell me that this is not a dream," said Irani, crying with happiness.

"My good brother, you don't know how happy I am at this moment! Tell us, what happened to you?" Jaci asked, hugging him affectionately.

"Well, it's a long story, but what I can say at the moment is that I was in a very faraway place…And that I only managed to come back and be with you again thanks to Tupa and, also, to these four friends of mine here present."

"Stop being modest, Uirapuru! Thanks to your efforts, humility, and courage, you were able to accomplish great things, especially when you saved the son of Emperor Pachacuti, using the bow and arrow with great technique!"

"I couldn't have done it without you, Child God…"

"You don't have to call me that, my friend!"

"Okay…I guess I'll call you Boy God then!"

When he saw that Mr. Acaua was teary-eyed and much moved, Uncle Alberto said,

"Now let's stop with this subject and think only about having fun."

"Cool! Let's go sing too," said Samuel, beginning to dance.

The party was getting so good that no one wanted to leave so early. And it was not for less, with so much abundance, good music, and nice people, there is no one who didn't like it.

This joy lasted all afternoon, but as they saw the sun begin to set, the indigenous people understood that it was time to go.

The old Indian and his family decided to stay just a little longer to help organize the mess. Not wanting to let that opportunity pass, the two brothers created courage ran to the house, and came back quickly bringing gold necklaces.

Uncle Alberto, who was a few steps ahead, delivered first to Jaci and Uncle Milton; then he delivered to Irani. Seeing that they had liked it, they left aside their shyness and coincidentally decided to ask them to start dating at the same time.

"Yes...I accept!" responded together as well.

Mr. Acaua, who was near and had heard everything, told them,

"I feel happy for this event...Since they were born, I wished that one day good-natured suitors could appear in their lives, regardless of whether they were from my tribe or not...You two are from an excellent family, you are educated and hard-working...That is why you have my permission and I hope you will be happy!"

Grandma Maria and Grandpa Jorge, who were passing by and heard part of the conversation, were also very happy and praised the ladies equally. Finally, everyone said goodbye and closed that day with many joys.

***

A few days later, on a beautiful sunny morning, the boys heard a noise coming from the gatekeeper. As they approached, Allan was soon screaming with happiness.

"Mom! I missed you so much!"

"I too did miss you, son!"

Grandpa Jorge who was just behind, holding the key to the lock, smiled and said, "What a good surprise, my child! Wait just a little longer; I'll open the gate...And who are those with you?"

Julia, only after giving a strong and affectionate hug to everyone, answered the question:

"I met this nice couple at the bus station and when they told me they were coming this way by car, I took the ride...They are new around here. They just bought a property right up ahead..."

"That's great! Welcome, and good luck."

"Thank you, Mr. Jorge! We have learned that you are one of the oldest residents of these bands," argued the new neighbor.

"Yes, this is true!"

"Oh! Just to let you know, we are traders of farm products, our business is to buy and resell."

"So, you guys got lucky, my friend, because I have something you're going to like a lot," said Grandpa Jorge all excited.

"How nice! In a few days, we will come back to see what it is and, who knows, negotiate! Well, see you later. It was a pleasure to meet you!" completed the man.

"Likewise," responded with the greatest education to the people of the site.

As soon as they entered the house, Grandma Maria opened a big smile and hugged her daughter affectionately. They missed each other so much that the warm and long hug only ended when they heard Uncle Alberto and Uncle Milton approaching the house joyfully, knowing that the sister had just arrived.

As soon as the brothers entered, happiness was complete, because, at that moment, the family was all together and the best, everyone was very healthy, happy, and without any serious problem to solve.

At the end of the afternoon, everyone went to sit on the balcony to listen to a viola song and enjoy a tasty and plentiful snack. Little by little, they were catching up on conversations. After many reports, Julia, who was surprised by everything she had heard, said,

"You mean, after so many threats, you still figured out why they are interested in the place! Alberto and Milton were kidnapped, they managed to escape, they found a forgotten treasure inside a small cave, Colonel Faustino was arrested, his goons died…Ahh, and not to mention that I now have two twin sisters-in-law…Phew! This is sounding like a movie! Well, I think I'll go to my room to rest; for someone who is going to stay here only three to four days, I want to get up early and enjoy the farm a lot…Good night!"

"Good night," everyone replied.

***

The next day, everyone got up very early and excited. They even tried to do the tasks faster, because they knew that Julia wanted to enjoy the farm with her family. Finally, everything was prepared and tidy, and everyone went out for a picnic near the waterfall. The day was beautiful, so they took the opportunity to swim, fish, pick fruit, climb small trees and, all that, listen to beautiful songs played on the guitar by Grandpa Jorge, also accompanied by several birds.

The last days of the children's vacation were also like this; happy and fruitful, especially on the last day, when they had the presence of Jaci, Irani, Uirapuru, and Mr. Acaua.

At the end of the day, Julia packed her bags and the boys' bags. He decided to leave at that time because he wanted to arrive early in Sao Paulo and have at least one day to rest before classes restarted.

***

The farewell was the biggest sadness, because Grandma Maria and Grandpa Jorge cried a lot seeing their daughter and the boys, who made the house so happy, go away.

"Don't cry, Grandma…Don't be like that, Grandpa! Soon we will be back, I promise!" said Allan embracing them both, accompanied also by Samuel and Julia.

As soon as they got on the wagon, Uncle Milton said,

"Wait just a little longer, Alberto, I'm forgetting to pick something up!"

Three minutes later…

"Take this bag with you, Samuel and give it to your father! Allan commented to us that he is unemployed…Surely, this will help him a lot."

"But, Mr. Milton, this bag is one of those with the jewels! You will need this to pay…"

"Don't worry! We've separated enough for us, not to mention that the couple who brought my sister here bought and paid in cash for our crops."

"Great! I'm glad about that!"

"I know! So, stay calm and take the bag, because it will help your family a lot."

"Thank you very much, Mr. Milton!"

"No need to thank me; you have a right to that too! Well, let's go soon; we have a good piece of ground until the bus station."

Allan, before going, hugged his grandparents once again, and, as soon as he looked up at the sky, he saw a big round light moving everywhere as if he wanted to say goodbye too. As soon as he saw it follow toward the mountain, he got on the wagon and left.

Chapter XIV
The Return to School

The return trip was very tiring and lasted the whole morning. As soon as the sun came up, they realized they were a few meters from the Sao Paulo bus station and soon they saw Mr. Richard Smith waiting anxiously for his family.

Allan got off the bus and immediately ran to hug his father, accompanied by his friend.

"What a nice hug, my son...I did really miss you!"

"Yeah, me too!"

"Mr. Richard, I loved the trip and...Oh...Sorry! First, good morning!"

"Good morning to you too, Samuel! I'm glad you liked it and I'm sure your parents will be even more so! And speaking of them, tell Mr. Paulo that I have good news for him!"

"Cool! As soon as I get there, I'll tell them!"

"Well, then let's go home soon...I can't wait to take a shower, eat something, and rest a bit," said Julia, giving her husband a kiss and a hug.

***

Later, after resting, Allan took his school supplies and started doing the science and history task that the teacher Telma had requested.

Joining what he had learned at school with what he had learned and experienced during the vacations, he got a rich topic to do a good job. However, regardless of this, he would have to work hard, because all the students in his class wanted to improve their grades and only one would win the prize of having fun in the best park in the city.

When the day came for the return to class, most students hugged each other cheerfully and smilingly for being reunited, and a minority was crestfallen and sad that they had finished their vacation.

Samuel didn't even make it to school, so he ran to his best friend.

"What's up, Allan, what's up?"

"Yes…And you?"

"Today I am very, very happy!"

"Will you…just say the reason?"

"His father went home yesterday at the end of the day and…"

"He went! I didn't even see him leave…Of course, I must have blacked out! But what about it?"

"And that's when he invited my father to work…"

"Wow, that's great!"

"From what I could hear, your father closed some contracts in London and will start exporting clothes there!"

"Really? I haven't had time to talk about it with him yet."

"Yes! And the best is that they will be partners! Those jewels, as far as I know, are worth a lot of money and with that, my father will invest even more in the making of his family."

"That's good, Samuel! My father and I are very fond of Mr. Paulo."

"Thanks, buddy! And then, did your mother ask you anything about this bracelet?"

"Sort of…I told her he came in the middle of the jewels and ended up staying with me!"

"You did well! But changing the subject and the school assignment were you able to do it?"

"Yes and…"

At that moment, Allan was mute and didn't even finish what he was saying.

"What is it, friend?"

"Just talking about the assignment and look who's here!"

"Yes. It's the teacher!"

"Strange, Samuel, she is alone…Let's go and say hello to her."

"We don't need to; she is coming toward us!"

"Good morning, boys. How did your vacation go?"

"Well done!" The two boys responded together.

"And you Samuel did you like the farm?"

"I love it…I even want to go back again."

"The next time my friend Julia goes, I will go too!"

"It will be a pleasure, Telma teacher! And you, did you have a lot of fun there at Santos Beach?"

"Yes, Allan. However, Jessica got a bad cold on her way home and maybe she will have to stay the whole week without being able to come to school."

"Ahh…So, that's why your daughter didn't come! But what about the amusement park, will she be able to go?"

"Well, I don't think so!"

"What a shame," said Allan quietly.

"Listen, kids…It's the school's bells ringing! Let's go to the classroom now."

As soon as everyone entered and sat down at their desks, the teacher Telma asked:

"Raise your hand that did the science and history research I asked for!"

Immediately everyone raised their hands making, also, a sign of positive.

"Mine must have gotten better! I know perfectly well that I am the smartest of the class!"

"Stop being arrogant, Jader! The whole class has potential! Well, I'll collect the assignments and only give the answer at the end of the week…Ah, I'll choose two students to take to the park, because my daughter won't go."

"Ahn…Damn! Just now she would have the opportunity to get to know me better…Surely, she would love me!"

"Quiet, Jader. If you don't behave, I will give you zero at work!"

"O…okay!"

***

It seemed like the week took a month to go by and, finally, when Friday arrived, everyone in that class was anxious and nervous to know which two lucky winners they would win.

As soon as the teacher entered the class, there was a general silence; only one voice didn't stop, giving the impression that the person didn't give a damn.

"I can't wait to get my ticket. And since my love won't go, I hope that one of you two will go with me," said Jader to friends Joca and Fred.

The teacher Telma pretended she didn't hear because she didn't want to have to stay every day and every hour drawing the attention of one or the other ill-mannered student. Only after she finished teaching her class, she took both tickets out of the bag and said, "Dear students, I will now say the names of the two people who did the best work. But first I would like to say that everyone did well. Probably during the year, there will be other challenges like this one and whoever does not win this time can win next time."

"Phew…I'm glad we're going to have other challenges because this time I know I lost! I thought it was to research the history of science…"

Joca was red with shame.

At this time, everyone laughed, and only after the teacher continued to speak did, they shut up.

"Well, as I was saying, I analyzed everyone's assignments, but two of them caught my attention! Although they approached the same subjects, I know they did not copy each other because each one explained in a different way…They reported very well on the fauna, flora, and ores of our country. I liked very much the explanation of the importance of uranium, which unfortunately is used in bombs, but is now a strong ally in obtaining electrical energy. I thought it was great the topic they approached about genetics, such as the cure of hereditary diseases, cloning of living beings, and cloning of organs for transplants…But what I liked the most were the history topics. Besides mentioning several prehistoric animals, they spoke very naturally about the city of Rome in 80 AD, ruled by Emperor Titus Flavius, the inauguration of the Coliseum, and the gladiatorial battles…The impressive thing was when they reported about the Inca Civilization in Cusco and the sacred city of Machu Picchu…It seems that they were even there and met the great Emperor Pachacuti and his son Tupac Yupanqui! So, for all that, the first winner is…"

"Congratulations, Jader! I didn't know you were so smart," said Joca, proud of his friend.

"Shut up, moron! I didn't even come close to this!"

"It's…Allan Smith. Congratulations, it was a great job! Come here in front to get your ticket."

"Thank you, Ms. Telma."

"And the second winner and can also come here to pick up his prize is…Samuel."

"Cool! Thanks a lot."

"Well, tomorrow we will meet. The place and the time are written on the back…So, let's go that the bells have already rang! Have a great weekend."

As soon as the teacher left the classroom, Jader met with his two friends and told them,

"Listen well…We can't let these two stuck-up guys have fun! We must do something to get in the way, understand?"

"Yes, you can count on me," Fred said.

"I was able to read on the back of Samuel's ticket the name of the park and the time agreed!"

"Well done, Joca! Then tomorrow we will be waiting for them," decided Jader.

***

The next day, the trio got up very early and met at an agreed point.

"Why did you choose this place?" Fred asked.

"Here's the thing…Yesterday, after class, I was around and I analyzed the path Allan will probably take from his house to the park…And, for sure, he will pass by here!"

"Yes, but what is your plan, Jader? And why did you bring buckets with fat? It smells strong!"

"Pay close attention, because I will not explain again! Here's the deal…I've concluded that it's no use trying to hold on to those two 'smugs', they are very smart and agile. If they manage to escape, they will have fun, and worse, they will mock our faces!"

"Yes, but what about it?" Joca asked.

"The only way to stop them is to make them embarrassed and ashamed, so they won't have the courage to proceed."

"Yeah, but it counts right away! What are you up to?" Fred was curious.

"Well, yesterday I got with an acquaintance of mine, owner of a restaurant in the corner of my house, these broths of meat and chicken leftover…My plan is the following…"

"Go on; explain immediately that I am very anxious!"

"You see those two trees in the middle of the block?"

"Yes," responded the two friends.

"That first one is right in front of a railing gate, where you can see three ferocious dogs that always seem to be hungry. You, Joca, will be hiding behind it…The other one is about ten meters later. Fred and I will stay hidden there, holding these buckets."

"But why do I have to be alone in the first tree?"

"It's very simple, Joca! As soon as those two passes and you see that all the broth has been thrown and spilled, release the brave dogs immediately…As soon as they are released, they will feel the strong smell of food and put them both to run."

"Oh, my God! Open the gate to the wild dog at the time of the spilled broth…My goodness, what a mess!"

"There's nothing confusing, Joca…Look, they're coming from up there. Hurry up, let's be ready!"

A few minutes later, Allan and Samuel, who were well dressed for the occasion, approached the trees, and as they saw Jader and Fred holding those mysterious buckets, they became suspicious and tried to walk faster.

"Where do teachers Telma's little boys go so clean and smelly?"

"Don't play the fool, Jader! You know very well that we are going to the park," Samuel replied.

"No, were! Come on Fred, the time for revenge has come!" Allan immediately understood what they intended.

Then, more than quickly, he pointed to those huge buckets and made them spin high, spilling all that broth over the troublemakers.

Joca, seeing that entire situation and not understanding anything, said loudly,

"Spilled broth, release the wild dogs! Go on, your fleabags, bite them!"

"Jader, get that damn bucket off your head, and let's run! That idiot Joca let the dogs free!"

"My God, he's too dumb! Let's get out of here!"

As soon as they ran in front of the park gate, Fred shouted,

"Look, Jader, who's at the door!"

"Damn it! I hate Allan! One day he will pay for it!"

"Look, there's a stream up ahead! Let's jump in the water and get rid of this horrible smell and the dogs," said Fred, playing smart.

As soon as they jumped, Jader was almost crazy from screaming,

"You idiot! You and Joca are the same…This here is sewage water!"

Finally, the two winners of the best assignments arrived at the main entrance of the so dreamed park.

"Allan, look who's up ahead!"

"My goodness…I don't understand! It's Jessica!"

"Yes, and she's with her mother and another girl too!" Despite all the shyness, the two boys approached with a big smile stamped on their faces and immediately went greeting each other.

"Hello, how are you?" said both at the same time.

"Fine…" answered all three.

"I thought you wouldn't come, Jessica. I heard you were sick!"

"Yes, I got better yesterday, and I already feel a lot better today. I even invited my cousin Livia to join us."

"Ahh…How rude of me! I am so distracted waiting for a friend, that I didn't even introduce my niece to you. Livia, this is Allan, and this is Samuel."

"It's a pleasure! I heard about the fame of you two at school. You two seem to be very dedicated!"

"Thanks!" exclaimed Allan.

Samuel only expressed his gratitude seconds later. He was aloft, his heart was beating strongly, and his eyes were shining differently. Surely the little angel Cupid passed by there too.

"Thank you, Livia! You are very kind."

The girl looked deep into Samuel's eyes and with a beautiful smile thanked him for the compliment.

"Ahh…Good! My friend is coming…Now we can enter."

"Mom!"

"Yes, Allan, I invited her to keep me company while you have fun!"

"And I thank you again for the invitation, Telma. Nothing better than to spend the day with such nice people, even more with my son."

"And not to mention that you wanted to surprise him didn't you, Julia?"

"Yes…I just don't know if he liked it!"

"I loved it, Mom!"

"So, guys, let's go inside, I'm already 'freaking out' to have fun!" said Samuel anxious and all excited.

The park was huge and very beautiful, and the entrance guaranteed access to all the numerous rides.

Julia and teacher Telma went to have refreshments in the cafeteria and remembered some old cases. The boys and girls entered every moment in a different ride and gave several screams and laughs.

The day went by with a lot of euphoria, excitement, and a great dose of happiness. And only in the middle of the afternoon did they stop to go to the cafeteria to eat something. The meal was delicious, and the ice cream was even greater…It was so good that Samuel took three and it seemed that he even wanted more. But he was so eager to get back to the rides and have some more fun that he gave up asking for the fourth and went on saying, "What's up, guys? Let's go back and play more?"

"Samuel, if you want, you can go. I'm going to stay here just a little longer keeping my mom and the teacher company."

Jessica also said the same thing. Her cousin, Livia, agreed to go along.

"So, which ride are you thinking of going?" The girl asked.

"Until now, we have not been on the ghost train. What do you think?"

"I don't know…I think I'm going to feel scared!"

"Scared?"

"Yes, you don't?"

"To tell you the truth, I used to! But for some things that have happened to me recently, I have become braver!"

"Well, if you're saying I don't need to worry, then I will go!"

"Rest assured, Livia. You are with me, and nothing will happen to you, I promise!"

"Thank you!! I'd like to tell you that where I study I have practically no friends…I think I'll ask my mother to transfer me to your school."

"How nice…I love to hear that! But until then, I'd like to see you again…"

"Yes," answered the girl, smiling and looking at him with affection.

"Look, the cart has stopped. I think it's already our turn," said Samuel all happy.

A few minutes later, at the diner, Allan got up and called Jessica to go once more to the Ferris wheel.

"Yes, let's go!"

"Don't take so long, we'll only be here one more hour," teacher Telma spoke.

"Yes, Mom."

Not wanting to waste time, the two left quickly for the ride. It was clear that, at that moment, they were even happier to be alone.

As soon as they entered the Ferris wheel, each one's heart seemed to beat faster. Surely it wasn't because they were afraid, but because of the emotion of being close to each other.

"Look, Allan, those flowers down there. They look a lot like the one you gave me that day!"

"Yes, they are certainly the same."

"I loved it, it was beautiful! You have good taste!"

"Thanks! Maybe I do because it was there at school that I discovered the most beautiful flower of all…"

At that moment, the girl understood that it was a compliment; then she reddened herself for being a little shy, but she still returned with a beautiful smile. Then he looked the other way to see if his mother was still in the cafeteria. Taking advantage of the opportunity, Allan pointed to some flowers and made them come to his hand, without the girl noticing anything.

"Look, Jessica, what was hanging on beside the seat!"

"Wow…They are beautiful. I love it! But how did they get here? Coincidence, it even seems magical!"

"Yeah…Who knows!"

"Do you believe in this, Allan?"

"In what? In magic!"

"Yes, in magic!"

"I believe…The whole universe is made of mysteries…Beautiful things happen all the time. What we think is not real can be real. What seems to be impossible may one day be possible. One thing is certain: there is something in this life that is the greatest magic in the world and is called love! Nobody here needs superpowers, to be a superhero, or to have enough money to be happy…Just believe in yourself, have a good heart, help people, always follow the path of good, be polite, gentle, sincere, and…"

"I thought everything you just said was beautiful! But then, I want you to use your sincerity and tell me what was written in that letter!"

"Well, I think I can summarize it in just one sentence. But I remember I wrote that you are the most beautiful, graceful and kindest girl I have ever met. Your loving and special look, is the only thing that makes my heart beat strong when we meet…It's something sweet that I can't explain, but I know it makes me dream!"

"And what was the sentence you were going to summarize it all in?"

"I love you more than anything!"

"I love you too!"

Then, quickly, they held each other's hand, looked deep into their eyes, approached their faces, and finally…

Well, I think we'd better leave this beautiful couple at ease now, don't you?

end!